New Jersey Noir: Barnegat Light

NEW JERSEY NOIR:
BARNEGAT LIGHT

A Novel

BY

William Baer

ABLE MUSE PRESS

Able Muse Press

www.ablemusepress.com

Library of Congress Cataloging-in-Publication Data

Names: Baer, William, 1948 - author.
Title: Barnegat Light : a novel / by William Baer.
Other titles: At head of title: New Jersey noir
Description: San Jose, CA : Able Muse Press, 2021. | Series: The Jack Colt
    murder mystery novels ; book three
Identifiers: LCCN 2021024304 (print) | LCCN 2021024305 (ebook) |
    ISBN 9781773490991 (paperback) | ISBN 9781773491004 (ebook)
Subjects: LCGFT: Detective and mystery fiction. | Noir fiction. | Novels.
Classification: LCC PS3552.A3324 B37 2021 (print) | LCC PS3552
    A3324 (ebook) | DDC 813/.54--dc23
LC record available at https://lccn.loc.gov/2021024304
LC ebook record available at https://lccn.loc.gov/2021024305

Printed in the United States of America

Cover image: *Cornering* by Alexander Pepple

Cover & book design by Alexander Pepple

Able Muse Press is an imprint of *Able Muse: A Review of Poetry, Prose & Art*—at
www.ablemuse.com

Able Muse Press
467 Saratoga Avenue #602
San Jose, CA 95129

For my family and friends—

especially Rob

CONTENTS

New Jersey Noir: Barnegat Light

I

II

III

New Jersey Noir: Barnegat Light

I

New Jersey is the only state where the politicians are more corrupt than the mob.

— Thomas C. Colt

1. Brownstone

Tuesday, May 10th
58°

PATERSON ELECTED a new mayor tonight.

A murderer.

Trust me.

Meredith Hopkins, twenty-seven, mayor-elect, got seventy-two percent of the vote against six other hapless candidates. Did I mention that she's the daughter of the governor? Maybe that helped a bit. Along with a ton of outside money.

Tonight she's celebrating at the Brownstone on West Broadway, sipping champagne, surrounded by a million sycophants in the Grand Ballroom.

Beneath four chandeliers.

I wasn't there.

I was at home, sitting on my couch, watching *Jaws* and rooting for the shark.

A few years ago, we went on two dates (me and Meredith), both dumbass mistakes on my part, before she started killing people. She was raised right here in beautiful Paterson, back when her old man was the sitting mayor. She was irredeemably spoiled by both of her parents (both of whom she naturally detests) along with her bratty little sister, who was psychopathically deranged, now deceased, whom she also detested. Having said all that, there's no denying that Meredith is smart, ambitious, articulate, and attractive.

Very.

Eddie Ravello once looked at her and said:

"That one's hotter than sunstroke."

So I gave him a look.

He rephrased:

"That's a *very* lovely young lady."

I never cared for all that "hot" crap, even when the women say it. About guys. About other women. I'm not fond of "sexy" either. So I guess I'm a prude, but I doubt anybody'll call me on it.

My uncle Tom raised me to respect women.

Unless they're pointing a weapon in your face.

Eddie, by the way, was the youngest son of Don Ravello, and Meredith had him assassinated a year ago. Not because he called her "hot." For other reasons. I knew it, the cops knew it, the troopers knew it, and the feds knew it, but she spent less than two hours in jail, made bail, and then, as she was waiting for the charges to get dropped, she decided to run for mayor.

Paterson mayors typically go to jail *after* they've been elected. At least two in the last two decades. Mostly for the usual "Jersey" stuff, kickbacks, extortion, corruption, etc.

I'm told she wore a slinky red Versace tonight, slit down to her navel. I'm exaggerating, of course. I'm sure Meredith looked, as they say, "perfectly stunning." Tallish, long, glossy jet-brown hair, Atlantic blue eyes, with, I'm certain, the reddest red lipstick on her red-red lips. Tomorrow, all the reports will say she looked "breathtaking." "Elegant." Maybe even "classy."

She mingled with the crowd. Hobnobbing, celebrating, sucking in the endless compliments, the fawning, the obsequiousness, occasionally chatting about "nothing much" with Governor Hopkins and his ever-popular First Lady, so proud of their high-maintenance, psychopathic daughter. Eventually, things wound down.

The ass-kissers started peeling off, and the ballroom was mostly empty. Slightly drunk, Meredith left the Brownstone with her two assistants, and her two bodyguards, one of whom, or both, was surely a "boy toy" for later tonight. They exited into a magnificent Paterson night. A bit cool, but perfect. Muscleboy number one opened the back door of her huge black limo. Meredith was triumphant, on top of the world. The mayor of the great city of Paterson, New Jersey.

As she turned to speak to Muscleboy number two, a shot rang out. Instead of perforating her heart, it cracked through the bones in her right shoulder. Terrified, she immediately dropped down behind the limo, as the two subsequent shots rang out, as each of her bodyguards slumped to the floor of the alley.

Then she did the inexplicable.

She pulled out her phone.

Guess who she called?

Me.

Roy Scheider is sitting on the beach and he sees the damned thing in the water. Then Spielberg, imitating Hitchcock, does a perfect dolly-zoom facing the police captain. It's a great shot, which was now being interrupted by an irritating phone call.

I hit pause and answered my cell.

"This better be good."

"Jack."

I'd know that voice anywhere, even on the beach on Amity Island with a shark loose in the water. Instead, it was another kind of shark, but she sounded different tonight, somehow off, probably drunk, maybe calling to gloat.

Her Honor, the mayor.

She clicked off.

I pushed it out of my mind.

I was enjoying the movie.

Relaxing.

I was, dare I use the word?, "happy." As I usually am, although no one seems to notice.

It might surprise you to know that New Jersey is one of the "happiest" states in the union. Number six, in fact. Minnesota is number one, but I think I'll stay right where I am.

A few years ago, WalletHub did a huge national survey based on twenty-eight key "metrics." In the "Emotional and Physical Well-being" category, New Jersey was third. (Hawaii was first, Arkansas was last.) Also of interest, in the "Lowest Share of Adult Depression," Jersey was second. (Again trailing Hawaii, with Oregon as the worst. What the hell's going on up there in Oregon?) Jersey was also number two in "Lowest Suicide Rate," and number three in "Lowest Divorce Rate."

Come to New Jersey and be happy!

We need more traffic congestion.

We need more people to overtax.

I fired up *Jaws* again.

Later, just before Scheider shoves the scuba tank down the shark's throat (I'd shifted allegiances by now), the phone rang again.

Pause again.

"What do you want!"

"Hey, grumpy."

It was my best friend, Luca Salerno, who was also chief detective at the Paterson Courthouse.

"The shark's about to get blown to smithereens," I explained.

Understanding my frustrations, Luca got right to the point.

"Meredith Hopkins was shot dead tonight, outside the Brownstone."

I didn't know what to say.

Luca continued.

"I guess the Ravellos took care of business."

I thought it over.

"You wanna come and look?" he wondered.

"Nah, I'll sit this one out."

He understood. We hung up.

I don't wish people dead.

But some deserve it more than others.

2. Pines Lake

Tuesday, May 10th
56°

I RACED THROUGH an upscale section of upscale Pines Lake, not far from Laurelwood Arboretum, then pulled up in front of a large, isolated, white-brick colonial. The front door was open. When I stepped inside the living room, the judge was hanging from the two-story vaulted ceiling. Beneath him, a pretty young woman was sitting on the floor, stunned, distraught.

She looked up.

At me.

It was a very sad face, but a beautiful one. She was wearing a dark green dress that looked black in the dimly lit room. Her shoes were off. She had big big hair, very thick and black, yet perfectly in place. She also had wet sorrow-eyes and wet disbelieving lips. In my racket, given my "cinema" background, I always make snap judgments about who people look like. It comes in handy.

The best I could do was the young Gabrielle Union.

She nodded across the room at the interior hallway.

"There's more."

"Don't move," I said.

"Down in the basement."

About twenty minutes ago, around midnight, I got my third interruption. Scheider and Dreyfuss had just done their business, and they were swimming toward shore.

"I used to hate the water."

The phone rang.

I picked it up.

Why not.

"Yeah?"

The voice was urgent.

"This is Savannah Garvey. My father told me to call you if I ever needed help."

It was clear that she needed help.

Right now.

"Where are you?"

She told me, and I came immediately.

Her old man, now hanging from the ceiling, was one of the most respected judges in Passaic County. Once a liberal councilman in Wayne, he'd become a hard-ass judge in Paterson. I'd only had a few dealings with the guy, but I liked him, and so did my uncle Tom.

I walked across the living room, into a lighted hallway, then followed a trail of blood deep inside the huge house. Eventually, I came to a large, reinforced, open doorway leading down to the basement. The blood continued down the stairs. The room down below was lit. Off in the far corner of the room, there was a cell. Yes, a jail cell. With iron bars. With a dead man lying inside. A smallish man who'd obviously been shot several times. I won't bother to describe all the blood.

Outside the cell, there was another dead man. Much younger, in a guard's uniform, with a holstered weapon and a bullet hole in his forehead.

Why was a distinguished judge hanging by the neck in his living room?

It's a fair question, but stuff like that happens all the time.

More curiously, why's he got a prison cell in his basement?

And why's there a guy inside?

And why's there some kind of "guard"?

And why are they both dead?

I like mysteries. I guess that's obvious given my profession, but this one was a good bit weirder than most.

Which I liked.

A lot.

I went back upstairs, sat on the living room couch, and dialed the Wayne police. The judge's daughter crawled onto the couch, put her head in my lap, and held me tight.

We waited for the cops, as I kept thinking about that old film by Juan José Campanella, *El secreto de sus ojos.*

3. Barnegat

T HERE'S AN odd-looking person asking to see you."

It was the ever-soothing voice of Mrs. Doris Salerno screeching through my intercom, obviously insulting a potential client who was sitting a few feet away from her in the reception room.

Mrs. S., "Nonna," was Luca's seventy-three-year-old grandmother, a former librarian, who's been "helping me out" both as a researcher and a receptionist ever since my, how shall I put it?, "girlfriend" packed her possessions into her little red Neon and drove as far away from me as possible last year. To California.

"Actually, she's kind of cute. She says she's with the FBI, but she looks like she's with the Girl Scouts."

I tried not to laugh at the rudeness of my rude receptionist.

"Send her in so I can buy some cookies and get rid of her."

I guess I'm a bit rude myself.

So what? It's New Jersey. Get used to it.

Besides, I don't care much for feds.

I'd spent the morning with the local cops in Wayne, most of whom I knew and liked. Now I was sitting in my office, hoping not to be disturbed.

dering what I was doing.

e waiting for the *El secreto* DVD to arrive

ding from my uncle's list of favorite "last words."

olt, my great-uncle, raised me after my parents died in

when I was ten months old. He taught me everything I

new about being a PI and everything I ever knew about being

man, about trying to be "decent." He was the best private dick

in New Jersey for several decades until he was murdered early this

year at the Paterson Falls, which I prefer not to dwell on right now.

He was also very well read, two books a week, for his entire life. He died at seventy, so you can do the math. He taught me to do the same thing. This week I'm reading *The Informer* by Liam O'Flaherty, but at the moment, I was reading from Uncle Tom's "Last Word" list, from his "Humorous" section:

> *"The governor just lost my vote."*—Christopher Scott Emmitt, executed for murder in 2008

> *"How are the Mets doing today?"*—Moe Berg, former MLB catcher and American spy

> *"She still fascinates me."*—Richard Burton, thinking of his twice-married wife, Elizabeth Taylor

> *"My mother did it."*—Arnold Rothstein, underworld bookmaker, fixer of the 1919 Black Sox Scandal

> *"I wish I'd drunk more champagne."*—John Maynard Keynes, misguided economist, right-minded champagne drinker

I don't drink much, but who doesn't like champagne?

The "odd-looking person" entered my office. She was slight, maybe five foot two, delicate, ethereal, youngish, but cute. She had soft blonde hair, horn-rimmed glasses, and *very* distinctive, very fascinating orange eyes. What they call "amber." She was wearing a boring dark-blue FBI pantsuit, and she looked like a bookish "desk" type.

Overall, a bit nerdy, a bit mousy.

Later, when I Googled the word to make sure it wasn't too pejorative, Webster said that it means "timid," "diffident," "like a mouse."

I thought it meant "cute as a mouse."

Let's stick with that.

So who does she look like?

Maybe Eva Marie Saint as young Edie in *On the Waterfront*? Which seemed perfectly appropriate since Eva Marie was a Jersey girl from Newark, and the classic film was shot in Hoboken.

I waited for her to sit down. She didn't. Yeah, she was slight, but she was focused.

On a mission.

She paid absolutely no attention to the countless framed photographs covering my walls. Photos of famous NFL linebackers and photos of famous New Jersey singers.

From Sinatra to Whitney.

She placed a copy of today's *Star-Ledger* on my desk.

"I want you to find the killer."

She had a lovely voice.

"Sounds good to me."

I quick-read the circled article about a young woman found dead and oddly mutilated yesterday down at the Shore. At Barnegat Light. She was a twin.

I assumed the dead girl's twin was standing patiently across my desk.

I like twins. My uncle Tom was a twin, being the twin brother of my long-dead grandfather, and last year, I got caught up in a case involving twins, known in the press as "The *Killing* Killing," due to the similarities with the television show.

I looked up.

"Why don't we go to Barnegat?"

She was pleased.

To be honest, I was hoping to get involved in Judge Garvey's hanging, especially given the weirdo business about the "prison cell" in the basement, and the dead "inmate," and the dead "guard." But I needed to be hired by someone in the family, and it hadn't happened yet.

Instead, I was off to the Jersey Shore.

With Special Agent Zoe Hathaway, who didn't drive anymore, ever since a smashup on the DC beltway last year. Earlier, she'd Ubered all the way from Barnegat to Paterson, 110 miles, so we drove back together in my black XTS.

A Vsport with a 410-hp twin turbo.

I took 19 south into the Parkway.

Since she's not much of a talker, I asked her a lot of questions.

"Why me?"

"You know the answer to that."

It wasn't dismissive, but she was definitely right. Why not me? I had an inflated rep in the metro area, especially for "solving" the "Barrens Kidnapping," "The Little Girl Murders," and a year ago, "The *Killing* Killing," which also took place down the Shore.

In Cape May.

"You seem to get things done," she added.

I liked the comment, but I changed the subject.

"You identicals?"

"Yes."

"Close?"

"Very close. *Very*. When I got reassigned to DC last year, it was a killer for both of us. We talked on the phone every single day."

"Yesterday?"

Meaning before her sister was murdered.

"Yes."

"About what?"

"Sister stuff. Work. The beach. Her new boyfriend. Getting together tomorrow at the beach house. We were very excited about it."

"Was anything bothering her?"

"No."

Out of nowhere, she went soft, and I thought she might start crying, so I changed the subject.

"What do you do in the Hoover Building?"

"I'm a liaison with NIPRCC, the National Intellectual Property Rights Coordination Center overseen by Homeland Security."

It sounded boring as hell.

"That's a mouthful."

She dumbed it down.

"Piracy. Intellectual property. Mostly cybertheft. Films, books, games, music, and apps. I'm in the books unit. About twenty percent of the e-books read online are pirated through illegal file-sharing websites. Overall, it's a billion-dollar business."

"You like it?"

"Most of the time. But it's hard to shut them down. Many are overseas, and they always come back again in a variant form. It's like whack-a-mole."

"Sounds frustrating."

"Yeah, but crime never ceases, right? I'm sure you know something about that, Mr. Colt."

I liked her, but not the "Mr. Colt" business.

"Call me Colt."

"Yes, Mr. Colt."

I looked over, and she smiled. I liked her smile. It drew attention away from her gigantic, nerdy horn-rims.

Then she put her head back and snuggled into the front seat. Which is easy to do when you're about five foot two, probably ninety-five pounds.

"I'm shot," she explained.

It was one of my uncle's favorite expressions.

She looked beat. Exhausted. Her sister had been murdered yesterday morning, and she probably hadn't slept a bit last night.

"Shut your eyes," I suggested.

She did.

"Could you stand some music?"

"Maybe. What kind?"

"The Boss."

"Of course."

I hit a button and my CD continued, starting with "Jersey Girl," which might be my favorite Springsteen. Certainly top three.

Yeah, I know, it's a cliché.

A Jersey guy who likes the Jersey rocker, especially a song called "Jersey Girl." But I've got no problem with it. I fit into a whole bunch of clichés. Who doesn't?

> *Tonight I'm gonna take that ride,*
> *Across the river to the Jersey side*

I was already on the Jersey side.

Tom Waits wrote the "crooner" for his Jersey girlfriend, and the song's been much discussed because the Jersey girl in the song isn't exactly the Jersey Girl stereotype.

Who cares?

Jersey has all kinds of girls, all of them lovely.

Down around Red Bank, my cell went off.

I muted the Boss.

"Colt."

It was Savannah Garvey.

Finally.

"I want you to find the killer."

"The Wayne cops are more than competent."

"I know that, but I want you to look into it. Into everything."

Meaning the jail cell and its occupant.

"I'm working another case down at the Shore."

"Then do two."

I remember that my uncle once said:

>   *"Only an idiot takes two cases at the same time."*

I was about thirteen back then. A doubting wiseass.

"How many times have you done it?" I asked.

He laughed.

"Three times."

"Did you make it work?"

"Yes."

"I'll do my best," I told Savannah, hoping I was half the man my uncle had been.

"Fine."

"How are you holding up?" I asked stupidly.

"A wreck. When are you coming back?"

"Late tonight. Tomorrow."

"Thank you, Jack."

Only my closest friends, and a few enemies, call me "Jack," but she said it with such sincerity that I didn't have the heart to correct her.

I'll clear it up tomorrow.

We hung up.

Zoe was semi-sleeping, partially listening.

"It won't affect your sister's case," I said, wondering if it was a lie.

I guess my so-called "reputation" gave it an air of verisimilitude.

"Fine," she said sleepily.

I took Exit 63 to Route 72 over the Henderson Bridge, then headed north on Long Beach Island.

Beautiful Long Beach Island.

Old Barney, the famous Barnegat Lighthouse, sits at the northern end of the island.

Back in 1609, Henry Hudson was the first to go snooping around Barnegat Bay. Over the years, its powerful tides created numerous shipwrecks and tons of erosion. But you can't "undo" the beautiful. After the original lighthouse collapsed into the ocean in 1857, they brought in an Army engineer, Lt. George Meade, who would later win the battle of Gettysburg, to build a new one. It was commissioned in 1859 with a twelve-foot Fresnel lens, and the tourists still love the place. Old Barney, red on its top half, white on its bottom half, can be seen on tons of New Jersey license plates.

Fortunately, Zoe wasn't the one who found the body, but the cops had told her the "where" and the "how," and I wanted to check it out. I pulled into the parking area. Then we walked to the front of the lighthouse. Tourists were lurking here and there, but not at the front, so Zoe walked over to the entrance. She sat down, facing outward, crossed her legs at the ankles, then rested her forearms on her thighs and intertwined her fingers.

It looked like some kind of yoga position.

"This is what Gallagher told me," she said.

Referring to the lead detective on the case.

"She was sitting upright, with two words marked across her forehead. 'NOT HER.' With some kind of black marker, maybe a Sharpie. And her eyes were damaged."

"How?"

"He wouldn't tell me."

I looked into Zoe's amber eyes, which even behind the silly glasses, glittered oddly in the New Jersey sun.

"Anything else?"

She shook her head and stood up.

In the *Star-Ledger* article, it said that the body was discovered by an early morning dog-walker, a local guy.

"Anything about the dog guy?"

"Just some harmless local carrying an excrement bag."

I wanted to laugh, but it didn't seem appropriate standing a few feet from where Chloe's dead body had been killed and mutilated, but I certainly appreciated the little fed's sarcasm. I guess she wasn't a dog person.

Neither am I.

She looked at me. "Up" at me. I'm a foot taller.

"Take me to the morgue."

4. Morgue

SHOULD YOU wait outside?" I wondered, attempting to be sensitive.

We were standing outside the entrance to the Ocean County Morgue in Tom's River.

"No."

We went inside. The ME, an older, seemingly competent, gray-haired woman in her sixties, was waiting next to the table. Chloe Hathaway's head was protruding from a white sheet. Her face was colorless, but, except for that and the glasses, she was an exact copy of the young woman standing beside me.

Her eyes were closed.

"NOT HER" was marked across her forehead in black lettering.

When prompted, Dr. Richter explained her suppositions.

Chloe was tased in the shoulder. Then a knife, never found, was driven upward under her chin, deep into her skull, leaving her face oddly intact. The bleeding was profuse. At the time, Chloe was wearing pink beach shorts, a sports bra, a red "Emerson" T-shirt, and soft leather moccasins. She was probably killed where she was found. When she was dead and properly posed, her forehead was marked and her eyes were mutilated.

"How?"

"Punctured."

"How?"

"I don't know. Maybe a pen knife, maybe a letter opener."

"Let me see her," Zoe said.

The doctor, aware that Zoe was the dead girl's twin, looked at me.

Warily.

When I nodded, the ME pulled back the sheet. Entirely. Revealing everything, even the girl's feet.

Zoe looked at her sister without expression. Stoic.

Unembarrassed by her sister's nakedness, her exposure.

I pointed at Chloe's right hand, at the mark on her ring finger.

"It's a small silver ring," the doc explained. "Costume stuff. It's with her effects."

I looked at Zoe.

"From her boyfriend?"

"I don't think so. She told me she got a little ring from her boss's daughter. A young girl, maybe four or five years old."

I looked at Zoe.

"I need to see her eyes."

I was giving her a chance to leave the room.

"So do I," she said.

I nodded at the coroner, who leaned over the naked corpse and lifted the dead girl's right eyelid. It was a mess underneath. The iris was crushed and oddly mutilated. The amberness was gone.

Zoe said nothing.

"The other one," I said.

The doc lifted the left eyelid. More of the same.

Then somebody came into the room.

He was a big guy, almost as big as me, but someone who eats a lot more twinkies and misses a lot more days at the gym.

Luke Gallagher was a detective at the Barnegat Township Police Department. I'd called him from the lighthouse, and he was good enough to meet us at the morgue.

He nodded to Zoe, and we shook hands.

"I grew up admiring your uncle," he said.

Which was the easiest way to get on my good side.

"That means a lot."

He smiled.

"You haven't done so bad yourself."

"Whatever I've done, my uncle taught me."

When I'd thanked the coroner, the three of us went outside.

"How you doing?" he asked Zoe.

It was the same dumb question we all have to ask sometimes. A few hours ago, I'd asked Savannah Garvey the same thing.

"Holding up," she said.

So we talked about the case.

"I don't have a clue," he admitted. "She had no enemies, and given what happened, it can't be random."

"No locals?"

"Nothing."

"What about New York?"

Chloe worked at Random House in the city, and I knew that Gallagher had gone there this morning.

"Nothing."

"No leads? No angry writers? No jealous coworkers?"

"Nothing."

"What about the boyfriend?"

"He's all I've got, Colt, but the guy's barely coherent."

I liked Gallagher. He wasn't a "turf" cop. He was a serious cop who wanted to put bad guys in jail and didn't seem to mind me snooping around.

When we left Toms River, we drove to the beach house. At one point, we passed a field with two cowgirls on horseback.

"We used to ride," Zoe said, as if to no one.

I was surprised.

"I took you for the bookish type."

"I am, but we've been riding since we were kids, and I've seen every single western ever made."

Which I doubted.

"What's your favorite?"

There was no hesitation.

"*Shane.*"

I was impressed,

"Great film. In my top five."

"Along with what?"

I rattled off a few.

"*Stagecoach, Red River, High Noon, The Wild Bunch, The Good, the Bad and the Ugly.*"

"That's six."

I laughed, but I was getting nowhere.

"Tell me about Sykes."

The boyfriend.

The *new* boyfriend.

She shrugged.

"They met about a month ago. We're not exactly 'hot-and-heavy' types, but Bryan seemed to change things for Chloe. She was *very* excited about their relationship and very excited about getting us together at the beach house tomorrow."

I wondered if the one sitting next to me was envious of the other one. The dead one. The carbon copy.

I pushed it from my mind.

"Did you ever talk to the guy?"

"Twice, on the phone. Briefly. Chlo put him on."

"Tell me."

"Both were weird. The first time, he said, 'What are you doing?' Which seemed like a rather stupid question. Then the next time, two days ago, he asked me if I was wearing any jewelry."

"Which sounds equally stupid."

"Exactly."

Driving into Barnegat, I turned right off Central at Fourteenth Street, then drove down to the ocean. She pointed at an isolated, very attractive, brown bungalow. What some people call a captain's cottage.

It was cute, like her.

It was also where she and her sister had grown up, staring at the endless blue ocean.

There was no car in the driveway.

"He's not here," she said, disappointed.

He'd told her he'd be waiting for us, and I didn't like the look of it.

I parked, and we went inside. It was smallish, cozy, beachish, and neat as a pin. Lovely. With a large picture window facing the Atlantic.

"You want some lemonade?" she asked. "I'm all dried out."

"Sure."

She went off to the kitchen, and my cell went off.

"Colt."

It was somebody I didn't want to hear from, but I did my best to be civil.

I was standing in the little hallway of the cottage, and I stared at myself in the mirror.

Mirrors don't lie.

I was talking on the phone with a gangster, and the guy staring back at me in the mirror looked like one of his flunkies. Armani dark suit, navy, button-down, skinny black tie, dark Ray-Ban shades, with jet-black hair greased straight back. He looks like an extra in *Goodfellas*. Actually, he could have been one of the leads.

I looked at his face, my face, which I seldom did. Not exactly handsome, always observant, watching, taciturn, with enough of "something" to make the girls take a second look, maybe to check out the cross-like scar on his forehead. I guess I'd have to admit that I look kind of scary, kind of creepy.

Maybe I was creeping out little Zoe.

I hung up the phone.

She came back into the living room with two glasses of lemonade and handed me one.

As if I was a regular guy.

5. Sinatra Park

I WAS STANDING in Sinatra Park.

Waiting for the don.

The mob don.

Maybe it was appropriate.

Don't get me wrong. I love Frank. I listen to him all the time, but it would be less-than-honest to ignore his mob connections. Everybody knows that Willie Moretti of the Genovese family put a gun to Tommy Dorsey's head as he signed the release from Frank's singing contract. Which Puzo and Coppola reimagined for *The Godfather*. There's also no denying that Frank was down in Havana in 1946 drinking Mojitos with Lucky Luciano. And who hasn't seen the pictures of Frank in Vegas, or was it Tahoe?, with Sam Giancana?

I hummed a few bars of "New York, New York," to clear my mind, then looked across the river at the second greatest city in the world. (After Paterson, of course.) Sinatra Park, naturally, is located in Hoboken, where the chairman was born, not far from Pier A. It's got a soccer field, a running track, a gazebo, and a Roman-styled amphitheater. The state of New Jersey has countless great views of the city across the Hudson, and this is one of the best. The greatest skyline in the world. I settled on midtown. On the Empire State.

I heard footsteps.

"You looking for the ape?"

Meaning King Kong.

I'd never heard the don try to be funny before.

Something was up.

I turned around and looked downward at the most powerful man in North Jersey. He was early-to-mid-sixties, wearing shades and a much-too-heavy-for-May overcoat, looking like Richard Conte.

Don't they all?

He'd called me earlier at the Hathaway beach house when I was staring in the mirror at myself.

"Meet me in Sinatra Park."

Not "Please, meet me." Not "Could you meet me?"

"Why?"

He answered my "why" with a "when."

"At seven."

He hung up.

Yeah, something's definitely up. The don seldom, almost never, leaves the boundaries of Paterson, and tonight he was all alone, with only his driver, who waited beside the black Town Car and never said a single word.

Or made a sound.

The don, no-nonsense, got right to business.

"I hear you're mucking around in the Garvey case."

"I never 'mucked around' in anything," I assured him.

He ignored me.

"Last week the judge had dinner with a Rutgers law student named Angela Rossini. I think she might be searching for her father, and I want you to keep her out of it."

I stared through my shades into his.

"Why me?"

"Because I trust you."

"You shouldn't."

He said nothing, as immobile as the Sphinx.

"Who is she?" I asked, wondering if she was one of his bastards, even though the don never had a rep for running around.

"She's Eddie's kid, but she doesn't know it."

The mention of Eddie made me uneasy, which is normally an alien sensation for me. Eddie was the youngest, most likable, but "idiot" son of Francesco Ravello. We were quasi-friends growing up in Paterson. Last year, I was sitting next to Eddie when he was gunned down by one of Meredith's "paramours." Naturally, I've always felt bad about it, especially since the bullets were meant for me. I assume that the don believes I owe him one.

I looked at him hard.

"Did you kill Garvey?"

"No one talks to me like that."

"I just did."

He almost smiled, another rarity, then he decided to answer my question.

"No."

I was on a roll.

"Did you kill Meredith?"

"No."

There was a long pause.

"Unfortunately," he added.

Everyone in North Jersey expected the Ravellos to get their revenge on Meredith sooner or later. It made no difference that she was the daughter of the governor. She was "marked," and everybody knew it.

The don reached inside his coat pocket and pulled out a thick envelope. He tried to hand it to me.

"I'm not taking it."

Maybe he took it as an insult, but he contained his umbrage.

"Eddie's dead because of you."

He said it coldly, matter-of-fact.

I couldn't disagree.

"I'll do my best," I said, "but no promises."

He put the envelope back in his pocket and walked away. When the Lincoln was gone, I found a bench, looked at the darkening river for a moment, then read Nonna's "report" on the Hathaway twins.

> *Zoe Marie Hathaway (age 25, FBI Special Agent):*
> *Twin sister of Chloe Marie Hathaway (deceased)*
> *Born and raised on the Atlantic at Barnegat Light, her parents ran Hathaway Books, a popular bookstore in Atlantic City, until it went under five years ago. Then the parents (Richard and Marie) moved to Albany, New York, to run a Barnes & Noble, the same corporation that probably drove them out of business. Along with Amazon. Before the move to Albany, they left the beach house to the twins.*
>
> *Zoe and Chloe, identicals, like their parents, seem very bookish, straight-arrow, academic, and shyish, but nevertheless still popular with the other kids in grammar school and high school. They were slackers in the athletics department, but they both rode horses, played volleyball, kayaked in the ocean, and read tons of books. Straight-A types. After high school, they went off to Boston together, on scholarship in Emerson's famous publishing program. After matching "summa" degrees, the girls moved to New York City, living together in an apartment on 29th Street. Chloe got an upwardly mobile job at Random House, where she's had a few nonfiction successes, particularly a Times best*

seller called (get this) Get Happy by some lady professor at a college I'd never heard of. (Why does anybody need to read a book about being happy?)

Her sister, Zoe, however, enrolled at NYU for a master's in criminal justice so she could join the FBI's Cyber Division. Apparently, it pissed her off that so many books get pirated on the web.

Miss Do-Gooder.

They've had a few boyfriends over the years, even a pair of guy-twins at Emerson, but nothing very significant. It seems they prefer to be workaholics. Until recently. Until Chloe ran into some guy named Bryan Sykes and apparently "flipped out." (I'm currently working on Sykes's background. Coming soon!)

Last year, when Zoe was unexpectedly transferred from the New York office down to DC, she even considered quitting rather than leaving her sister. But, in the end, she decided to go. (Duty calls.) They both arranged for some days off this week so they could meet at the beach house, so Zoe could meet Bryan Sykes, who was bringing along a friend, a Hackensack neurologist named Dr. Krish Singh.

Why would anyone want to kill one of these sweet, conscientious, boring girls? We need to crack this one, Johnny!

Behave yourself.

Love, Nonna

No one *ever* called me "Johnny."

I stared out at the Hudson again and tried, for a brief moment, or two, *not* to think about murder.

It didn't work.

6. Stone Tower

Tuesday, May 17th
55°

*Y*OU DON'T *need to be here tonight, John.*
Said the wizened hermit in his tower. Sitting back on his lumpy cot in his priestly blacks, with a bunch of ace bandages wrapped around his right ankle.

Monsignor John C. Colt, my great-great-uncle, a mere ninety-eight, is the very last, except for me, of our "Jersey line" of the Colt genealogy, who'd slipped on the tower stairs three days ago and sprained his ankle. As a result, the doctors confined him to his tower "cell," which he didn't mind at all. So I visited every day (or Nonna did) to bring him sustenance (Broadway pizza, Subway sandwiches), along with some light reading, *De adherendo Deo* by Albertus Magnus, *Theologia moralis* by St. Alphonsus Liguori, etc.

Lambert Tower, seventy feet high, near the top of Garrett Mountain, was the companion piece to Lambert Castle. Yes, Paterson has a castle. Don't all American cities? It was built by one of the textile barons who were part of Paterson's great industrial past, initiated by Alexander Hamilton, which ignited the country's industrial revolution and changed the world. These days, the castle is a museum, and the tower, at least the room at the top, is the residence of a hard-assed old Jesuit who'd spent several decades trying to straighten out the mess at the Vatican, with negligible "tread-water" results.

Now he'd come home to die.

Did I mention he's blind?

Which is sadly ironic since the tower has spectacular views of Paterson, the New York skyline, Bear Mountain, the George Washington Bridge, and even the Verrazano Narrows.

It was almost midnight.

I was sitting in the room's only chair looking across the cot at my billion-year-old uncle.

Where else would I want to be?

Chasing women?

Like everyone else, the old man had a very distorted view of my love life.

I wanted to be here with you.

He seemed touched.

Thank you, John, that's kind of you to say.

He looked up at nothing, thinking.

All right then, entertain me.

I was ready.

How about a love story?

He hesitated.

Are you in the story?

I laughed.

No.

Good. Proceed.

So I told him the story of Tory Blake and Bryan Sykes.

Forty-one years ago, a kid named Bryan Sykes was born in Wayne, New Jersey, to Edward Sykes, a park ranger raised in Highland Lakes, and Jeanine Sykes, a middle school teacher from Boonton. They'd met at Rutgers, married, then moved to Wayne.

Nine days later, Tory Blake was born in Culver's Lake, New Jersey, to Andrew Blake, a construction worker, and Debbie Blake, a department store clerk with an interest in the occult.

A year later, Andrew Blake abandoned his family and moved to Poughkeepsie, New York, and Debbie raised her daughter to believe that her father was dead.

Things are moving slowly.

I ignored the old goat.

Nine years later, when Bryan was ten, his mother died in a car crash on Ramapo Valley Road. A few months later, Edward and Bryan moved to Highland Lakes in Sussex County. In northwest Jersey.

I know where Highland Lakes is.

I paid no attention.

It's five lakes with seven beaches.

I pressed ahead.

The distraught boy and his distraught father seem to thrive in their new environment. With lots of camping, lots of trailing, lots of horse riding. Then it happened.

Finally.

Twenty-eight years ago, on May 13, Bryan was out exploring one night on his own, heading toward the summit of High Point, which I'm sure you know is the highest point in New Jersey.

The highest point in the Kittatinny Mountains.

It's not easy having a know-it-all uncle.

Isn't intellectual vanity a sin?

Yes.

Having resolved that, I continued.

But young Bryan is distracted by a distant campfire, which, of course, is illegal on the mountain at night, so he heads right toward it.

Will he ever get there?

Isn't impatience a sin?

A foible.

I didn't argue with the canon lawyer.

Finally, Bryan arrives at the site, and he finds a pretty young girl sitting all alone by the fire in a Girl Scout uniform, with her eyes "wet and gleaming in the flames." Naturally confused, Bryan asks, "What are you doing?" The girl says, "Waiting for you."

I like it.

He falls in love.

I like it.

Instantly. And she does the same.

Good.

Then Bryan texts his old man a lie about spending the night with one of his friends, and he and the girl sit by the fire all night and become soulmates.

Any hanky-panky?

No one uses that word anymore. Assuming that they ever did.

All right, wiseass, any sex stuff?

No.

Like Wuthering Heights.

Even better. Catherine Earnshaw, despite all her protestations, was always a vacillator, and Heathcliff was never in her class. Or going to be. But these two seemed to be made for each other, and they recognized it instantly.

How old were they?

Thirteen.

A bit young to decide one's future.

When did you decide to be a priest?

Thirteen.

The next day, Bryan tells his father the truth, and Tory tells her mother the truth, and both parents go with the flow. Later that year, when the house right next to the Blakes goes on the market, Bryan convinces his father to move to Culver's Lake. By then, the parents, Edward and Debbie have become close friends.

Sex?

I really don't know, old man, but it seems not. Just good friends. In the aftermath, they all seem to enjoy the "good" life, the good country life. Especially the kids. With endless outdoor stuff. Riding the trails, swimming Lake Marcia, helping with the Sunflower Maze in Sandyston, working Ventimiglia's Vineyard in Wantage. With some movies and bowling up in Port Jervis.

Then the kids convince Edward to build a "passageway" from Bryan's upstairs bedroom to Tory's upstairs bedroom in the Blake house.

The houses must be very close together.

They are.

Have you seen it?

Yes, it's weird as hell.

It's also a recipe for disaster.

Meaning pregnancy, but I wasn't about to give anything away. The old boy would have to learn to "sit there" on his little cot and listen to the story as it unfolds.

I continued.

I suppose that the parents probably figured, if something's going to happen, it's going to happen no matter what they do. Or don't do. Kids don't need a passageway to fool around; besides, they had a billion acres of forest surrounding them. But the parents did establish a few "rules." No sex. No racket. No back-and-forth after 11:00 p.m. They also told the kids that Edward would "close off" the passageway when they turned sixteen.

I love modern-day parenting.

This was twenty-five years ago.

Same thing.

So the kids go to school together. They do *everything* together. And they plan to go to Rutgers together.

By the way, what was the young girl doing on the mountain all alone?

She was up there with her Girl Scout troop, but she wandered off by herself, unnoticed until the following morning. She told her mother that she felt "compelled" to do it, and her mother, who was into all kinds of New Age mumbo jumbo, just shrugged her shoulders.

The old priest was thinking things over.

I sense a "turn" coming.

Yeah. Got that right.

7. Guest House

I WAS STARING at Yankee Stadium.

In its latest incarnation.

So was Luca.

It was huge, maybe two feet high, maybe four feet long, sitting on a wooden table in front of us. Beige, three-dimensional, obviously built to scale, and composed entirely of little wooden toothpicks.

"How many?" he wondered.

I shrugged, throwing out a number.

"50,000?"

I had no idea, of course. I'd seen pictures of such things before, but never in real life.

"Nah, at least 100,000."

Said the expert.

We were sitting in the living room of Travis Turner. In the small guest house behind Judge Garvey's home. Turner was the man found dead, by me, last night, outside the basement jail cell, wearing a prison guard's uniform.

The guy was my age, decent looking, apparently an orphan

from Totowa. His parents had died in a house fire when he was an
infant, after which he'd done OK in several foster homes in Passaic
County. He was mentally challenged from birth. Something had
gone wrong. Nevertheless, he somehow managed to get through
grammar school, did some vocational training, then got mixed up
with some loser house thieves who used him as a lookout. When
he ended up in Judge Garvey's court fifteen years ago, the judge let
him off easy, then hired him as a handyman on his property in Pines
Lake. Living alone in the little guest house, Turner took care of the
lawn, the garden, and the pool. He also ran various errands around
town, and sometimes chauffeured the judge. Eventually, he learned
to cook, and he started preparing occasional suppers for the family.

It seems that the kids always liked him, "just like an older
cousin," and he was always included in family get-togethers, like
birthdays, Christmas, Fourth of July, and many trips to the Bronx
to root for the Yankees.

He had, from all accounts, an easy disposition, never feeling
sorry for himself, for his incapabilities.

"The guy's brain was damaged," Luca said, "but look at this
thing."

Meaning Yankee Stadium.

I was already looking at it.

Just as amazed as Luca.

Earlier, Luca had told the Wayne cops to leave the door open,
and I got here about an hour ago, doing a thorough inventory of
the place, hoping it might lead to something.

It didn't.

Like me, Turner lived alone. Like me, he was oddly neat and
organized for a guy on his own.

I started with his closet, with his three other prison guard uniforms, which were obviously custom-made, modeled on the Sing Sing uniforms.

His kitchen was small, where he prepared meals for himself and the guy in the prison cell, who'd now been identified as András Papp, a Hungarian immigrant convicted of aggravated assault thirteen years ago. On the kitchen table, there was a stack of plastic cafeteria trays, and the refrigerator had a ton of eight-ounce cartons of milk, chocolate milk, and orange juice.

There were two bookcases. One was filled, as at my house, with DVDs. Mostly rom-coms and old comedies like *Laurel and Hardy* and *The Three Stooges*. Nothing violent. No porn.

The other bookcase seemed to be reading material for his prisoner, András Papp, who was actually the judge's prisoner. Books about European history, the American legal system, some devotional books, some hagiographies, and several shelves of books in a foreign language, surely Hungarian.

There was no computer in the guest house. No cell phone either. Just an old-fashioned landline dial phone. There were no photos of either parents or girlfriends. Just a few happy pictures of Turner with the judge and the kids. One at the ballpark, all wearing Yankee baseball caps and smiling.

His bedroom was like a kid's room, except for the neatness. I liked it. There was a giant poster of Derek Jeter on the wall, six Yankee bobbleheads on a small desk, and a copy of the New Testament on a night table.

No diary.

Nothing much useful.

Just an hour perusal through the now-dead life of a young man with assorted problems, who seemed to be doing the best he could.

"It's hard to believe, Jack."

I didn't bother to say "What?" I just waited.

"I always thought Garvey was the decent type, but he was using this poor guy. Getting Turner to do his dirty work."

"Was the gun loaded?" I asked.

"No. Why would you ask such a thing?"

I shrugged.

"What was it?"

"A Ruger SR22."

I shrugged again, then I pointed at Gate Number 2.

"It's not quite finished."

Luca stood up to leave, to get home to his family.

"It never will be, Jack."

He looked down at the couch, at me.

"You going to stare at that thing all night?"

"I wish I could, but I've got some movies to watch."

He rolled his eyes.

"Lock it up, Jack."

"Done."

My best friend left, out to the dark evening, leaving me in the residuum of the terminated life of Travis Turner.

It seemed terribly sad.

He was my age, living alone.

I wondered if someone sitting on my couch would feel the same way.

Then I got up and left for home.

8. *El secreto de sus ojos*

Wednesday, May 11th
64°

I REWATCHED THE film.

Then I watched the American version with Julia Roberts, Chiwetel Ejiofor, and Nicole Kidman. Not only is the remake much weaker overall, but they also messed with the plot a bit, especially at the end, making things worse.

Then I read a bunch of reviews of both films.

El secreto de sus ojos was a 2009 Argentine film, cowritten and directed by Juan José Campanella, which won the Academy Award for Best Foreign Language Film. It's about a judiciary agent, Benjamín Espósito, who tries to solve the brutal rape and murder of a young married woman, Liliana Colotto de Morales. It soon becomes clear that the murderer is a young thug named Isidoro Gómez, but before he can be arrested, Gómez disappears. A year later, Espósito discovers the husband of the dead woman, Ricardo Morales, sitting in a Retiro train station searching for Gómez. Morales admits that he comes to the train station every single day, and Espósito is powerfully moved by the young man's love for his wife and his determination to find her killer.

Spoiler Alert!

If you don't want to know the end of the movie, skip the next two paragraphs.

Eventually, Espósito learns that Gómez is obsessed with a soccer team called Racing Football Club. When Racing comes to play in Buenos Aires, Espósito and his assistant roam the stands in the stadium during the raucous match, searching for Gómez. They finally spot him, and, after a long chase, Gómez is captured. The killer is eventually tried and convicted, but then he's released for political reasons so he can work as an assassin for the Peronists. Seeking revenge, Gómez comes after Espósito and kills his assistant. Afraid for his life, Espósito is forced into exile in rural Jujuy Province.

In 1999, ten years later, Espósito, who's still haunted by the case, tracks down Ricardo Morales, the widower of the murdered woman who's living alone in isolation. Morales tells Espósito that he's at peace, admitting that, years ago, he captured Gómez and shot him in his car trunk. Espósito, after he leaves, is still uncertain about what Morales has told him, and he goes back to the isolated cottage, where he sees Morales carrying food into a small barn. Following him inside, Espósito discovers that Morales has constructed a prison cell in the barn and that Gómez is inside, bearded and decrepit looking. The audience, of course, wonders what Espósito will do. He's a man who's dedicated himself to justice in chaotic Argentina. He does nothing. He leaves things exactly as they are.

I guess it's pretty obvious why the film came to mind when I walked in Judge Garvey's basement and saw András Papp dead in his prison cell. It's not that I thought there was any direct connection between the film and the Garvey case, but I did wonder if one had influenced the other.

Probably not.

The film came out in 2009, and the American remake came out in 2015.

The original András Papp case was in 2003.

What of it?

Why do I even bother to mention it? Because in one of the reviews I read, in a journal called *Cinematic Times*, I read something odd. Something that caught my attention. My interest. The reviewer, a guy named Randy Telson, mentioned, almost in passing, that the films reminded him of an old short story, "The Reparation," which he described as a "more benign" take on the premise.

Benign?

I was intrigued.

I left Nonna a voicemail.

> *See if you can find an old short story called "The Reparation."*
> *I don't know the author.*

That should make an ex-librarian happy.

9. Stone House

C AN I come in?"

I was kicking myself for not checking before I opened the damned door.

It was Pamela Hopkins, First Lady of the Great State of New Jersey.

The "mourning" mother.

The mother whose recently deceased daughter Meredith always referred to as the "First Ho" despite the fact that, in the eyes of the general public, she was even more popular than her popular husband, the Governor of the Garden State.

From all accounts, she'd once been a stunning beauty, and she still was, looking more like thirty than her actual mid-fifties. With thick dirty-blonde hair, magnetic brown eyes, seductive moist lips, and the trim, voluptuous figure of a twenty-year-old. She also generated what would best be described as "heat." Emanating an undeniable ambiance of raw, rancid sexuality. A trait that she'd passed along to both of her now-dead daughters.

She was wearing black for the wake later tonight, maybe Ralph Lauren, a dress that would have looked stunning anywhere, at the Met, on Bourbon Street, on Beale Street, or mourning one's daughter.

"Well?" she pressed me, more amused than impatient.

I hesitated.

We've got a lot of history. All bad.

She was standing in front of Stone House, *my* house, on the top of Garrett Mountain overlooking the great city of Paterson. My refuge. My fortress of solitude. Where I grew up in a womanless household, raised by a great uncle.

I opened the door wider, and she stepped inside.

Make that, "sashayed" inside.

She looked around the living room, dark with dark woods and an old stone fireplace.

She looked at me, with a smile.

"I've never been inside the He-Man Woman-Haters Clubhouse."

I tried not to laugh.

But I was also relieved. The woman had once seduced my uncle, many years ago, and I was glad that it hadn't happened here. Now I won't have to call in the hazmat team.

She sat down on the couch like she owned the place, like she owned the entire mountain, the entire state.

"What do you want?" I said, trying to get things over with as quickly as possible. After all, I had two cases to solve.

"You already know what I want."

She was right. She wanted me to look into her daughter's assassination at the Brownstone.

"Not a chance," I said.

She looked at me again.

Radiating heat, radiating charm.

"Why should I?" I said.

"Because she loved you, Jack Colt."

"Meredith never loved anybody but herself."

Despite the harshness of the statement, the brutal summation of her daughter's life, the mother offered no defense.

"When she was dying, she called you on the phone."

"Yeah, to come and save her ass."

"What did she say, Jack?"

"She said, 'Jack.'"

"That's it? Just 'Jack'?"

"Yeah, then her phone cut off. If I knew she was in some kind of trouble, I would have done something."

"I know you would have, Jack."

"Look, let's not get too sentimental, Pammy. Everybody who ever knew her, who *really* knew her, hated her guts. Even you."

She didn't deny it.

She stood up, casually.

Everything the woman did had a sexual component.

"You'll do it anyway, Jack."

She said it with irritating confidence as if it was a foregone conclusion. The woman's self-satisfaction always crept under my skin.

But I didn't let on.

Never show the rattler you're rattled.

She glanced down at the couch, then checked her watch, then looked back at me.

"I've got some time to kill, Jack. Why don't you seduce me?"

"You're too old."

Which was a lie, the woman looked younger than me, and I'm thirty-two years old.

She laughed again.

I have to admit it's a contagious little laugh. A seductive mix of fun, heat, self-effacement, and sex.

"Besides," I said, "I'm celibate these days."

She did it again. The little laugh.

"That'll be the day, Colt," she said in a kind of sensuous whisper.

I walked to the front door and opened it wide for her to leave.

She didn't seem to mind. She walked across the room, then stopped in front of me.

"You won't be able to let it go," she said, meaning the murder, not the sex.

She kissed me on the mouth like I was the love of her life. Wet, sultry, electric.

Then she passed through the door, and I shut it behind her.

I make a living intimidating people, and I always have the upper hand. *Always*. But never with *that* woman.

I went into the bathroom and washed out my mouth.

With mouthwash.

Literally.

10. Paterson Chess Club

R uy López meets the Steinitz Defense.
Pretty classic.

The judge, casually dressed, was white, and some skinny kid, probably a college kid, was black.

I scanned the board. They were about twelve moves in, and the judge's position was already faltering, although I'm not sure he was aware of it.

Ethan Mackenzie was one of Judge Garvey's colleagues on the Paterson bench. Like Garvey, he's always had a stellar rep. But I happen to know, firsthand, that the guy's no saint, but I still liked him anyway. I liked his pretty daughter Maria a whole lot more until she did something foolish and got herself killed a few months ago. Which is another story.

A sad one.

At the moment, the judge was totally absorbed in the board in front of him, but I didn't have time to waste.

"Judge."

In unison, Mackenzie and his opponent looked up at me with understandable irritation. What in the world could possibly be worse than interrupting a chess match?

Nothing.

He realized it was me.

"Jack?"

"We need to talk. Now."

It wasn't a command, but it actually was, and he understood immediately. There could only be one reason why I'd be standing in the middle of a room full of active chess boards and spaced-out chess geeks.

The Garvey case.

He apologized to his opponent, who was about eight moves away from totally obliterating the judge's position, and we made our way across the large room, weaving carefully through the boards, the matches, the combatants, before exiting into an empty little "snack & coffee" room.

The judge, a trim, gray-haired man in his mid-fifties, sat back on the table and looked at me directly.

"It's a sad business, Jack."

Garvey and Mackenzie were *more* than colleagues; they were good friends.

Longtime friends.

"Savannah hired me."

"I know. She's a smart girl."

"Where should I be looking?"

"The cases, I guess. Excepting a handful of criminals, the man had no enemies."

"*Which* cases?"

"Carlos Cortez?" he suggested. "There were some ugly threats in the courtroom. Maybe Crenshaw. He's a vindictive scumbag."

I already knew about both cases.

The Wayne cops had done a good job keeping a lid on things. So far, there was nothing in the press about the "room" in the basement. Or the guy in the cage. Or the dead "guard." But yesterday morning Luca texted me:

The name of the guy in the cage is András Papp.

I remembered the name, even though the case was before my time, back when I was still in law school in Newark, so Nonna and I did some superficial snooping around.

Thirteen years ago, the wife of András Papp, a recent immigrant like her husband, was killed in a mugging in the Lakeview section of Paterson. The killer, some goon named Kevin Keldon, got himself hit by a car as he was fleeing the scene, dying two days later. The public soon learned that Keldon had a mile-long rap sheet and that his scumbag lawyer, a guy named Alex Fontaine, got him sprung from a murder rap in Rahway two months earlier on some kind of exclusionary rule.

Somehow, András Papp got ahold of an old Ruger, walked up to Fontaine on Ward Street, and shot him in the stomach. Fontaine survived, ending up with paralysis in his left leg and a permanent limp. In those days, Glen Garvey was an up-and-coming, hot-shot lawyer who shocked everyone by agreeing to defend András Papp. The trial was heavily publicized, and Garvey lost the case. He was accused by many of offering a "weak defense," and Papp got nailed with a twenty-five-year minimum. The next shock took place when Andrew Morris, an ambitious appeals judge at the time, who was eyeing the New Jersey Supreme Court, who understood the obvious public sympathy for Papp, overturned the case and set Papp free.

Mackenzie was no dope.

He knew even more than I knew he knew.

"Was that Papp in the basement?" he asked.

He seemed genuinely astonished.

My silence confirmed it.

"It makes no sense."

I wasn't about to argue.

"What did everyone think happened to Papp?" I asked.

"It was assumed that he'd had enough of America and went back to Hungary."

"What happened to Fontaine?"

"He's still at it. The last I heard he was working at the Bergen County courthouse."

"What else can you remember about the case?"

He thought it over.

"Papp had a brother who wrote Glen a nasty letter from Budapest."

"Did you see it?"

"Yeah, Glen showed it to me back then. It was a bunch of threats about how he bette' get his brother off. About what a good man his brother was. And so on. That kind of stuff."

"Anything else?"

"No."

"If you think of anything, call me."

"I will."

Then I changed the subject.

"What about Greco?"

He laughed.

"They ran into each other last week at Home Depot."

"Anything happen?"

"Nothing. Glen said it was very 'cordial.' They nodded politely at each other."

"What about Garvey's two kids? And what about Matt Harker?"

"They're great kids, Jack. They both idolize their father, and so did Harker."

Who was the judge's legal assistant.

"Anyone else?"

He shrugged.

"Not really, Glen was greatly admired."

"I know that, but then why'd he have a prison cell in his basement?"

The judge was obviously baffled by the idea.

"I've got no idea. It seems preposterous."

"I saw it. I also saw the dead guy locked inside."

Mackenzie shook his head, visibly disturbed. Maybe he was wondering if he really *wanted* to know the truth.

"Thanks," I said.

He nodded.

"Back to battle."

"That kid's kicking your ass."

He was genuinely surprised.

"Really?"

He looked at me mischievously.

"Any advice, Jack?"

I did have a few thoughts about his king-side rook, but I kept them to myself.

"Wouldn't that be cheating?" I said.

"Yes," he agreed, horrified by the idea, horrified by his own moral weakness.

He'd certainly had some other weaknesses over the years. For starters, he was one of the three known lovers of Pamela Hopkins.

"Take it like a man," I suggested.

He nodded, rose from the table, and started toward the door. Then he stopped and looked back into my eyes. Into my Ray-Bans.

"Why not let things play out, Jack?"

Meaning, why not let it alone, especially the prison cell in the basement.

"I'm not big on waiting for things to happen. You know that, Judge. I *never* procrastinate."

He knew it was true.

Actually, if I can sidebar for a moment, I have a problem

even understanding procrastination. Even as a kid, I could never comprehend why people put things off, especially things they'd rather not do. Why not just do it and get it over with? It was so alien to my own fundamental essence, to my own fundamental nature, as well as that of my uncle, that I naturally looked into it one time. Into the so-called "condition." But the stuff I found on the web seemed more concerned with blaming everything on depression, self-repudiation, quirks in the prefrontal cortex, and, of course, the "classic excuse" of modern times, low self-esteem. It all sounded like crap to me, but what do I know?

Well, I'll tell you what I *do* know. Putting things off is both irrational and irresponsible. It's lazy and it reveals a lack of willpower, which is the key to everything in this life. Right? Just do it, then you'll feel a whole lot better. It'll even elevate your "self-esteem."

I also learned back then, to my astonishment, that procrastination is one of the most common problems on the face of the earth. A bunch of studies of college-age kids indicated that somewhere between seventy to ninety percent consider themselves procrastinators. Whoa! What the hell's going on?

Maybe I should keep my mouth shut.

"One more thing," I said.

The judge halted his death march toward the battlefield.

"What about Meredith Hopkins?"

He shrugged again, as if it was perfectly obvious, as if he and everyone else in New Jersey law enforcement knew the answer but were perfectly helpless.

"Remember, Jack, the Ravellos *never* forget."

I returned his shrug.

When he was gone, speaking of the Ravellos, I took a quick look at Nonna's "Angela Rossini" report. About the poor young girl who was *actually* a Ravello and didn't even know it!

Angela Rossini (age 23, Rutgers Law student):

She's only twenty-three years old, so I haven't come up with much.

Adopted at birth by Stephen Rossini, a respected CPA, and Gloria Rossini, a local librarian. (I love librarians! Don't you, John-John?) Angela grew up in Caldwell in Essex County in a comfortable middle-class neighborhood. Seven years ago, her father died of congestive heart failure, and Angela went through a bit of a rebellious period. Nothing serious. Nothing involving the law, just driving her mother crazy. Then she got over it, graduated from high school, and went to Drew University for creative writing. She's now finishing up her second year at Rutgers Law in Newark.

She currently interns at the Innocence Project in Newark, and she's also been interning with Judge Garvey, probably hoping for a post-grad clerkship in Paterson. As you know, she's best friends with Savannah Garvey, also finishing her second year at Rutgers Law. They seem like an odd couple to me. Maybe they're "more" than just friends? (Pardon my groundless supposition.) They currently share a condo in Richardson Lofts on Columbia Street in Newark.

She's what my mentally challenged grandson calls an "EJG." Watch out, Mr. Colt!

It was time to meet the EJG.

11. Rutgers Law

Thursday, May 12th
72°

"I'M NOT sleeping with you."

She sounded pretty determined about it.

Being someone else misled by my false "reputation" as a lover-boy.

I was sitting in the mostly empty student lounge at Rutgers law, the oldest law school in New Jersey, the largest public law school in the country. Depending on your political perspective (*don't* tell me!), the school's had a number of highly "distinguished" or remarkably "disreputable" alums and profs, including Senator Elizabeth Warren, Senator Robert Menendez, and one-time prof Ruth Bader Ginsburg.

Enough of that.

Angela Rossini had strolled across the student lounge with a self-composure equal to that of Queen Christina on her triumphant entrance into Rome.

Without the Bernini couch.

Let me attempt to describe her.

Huge hair, not simply big hair, but huge. Black as night, teased, and lush. Purple eyeshadow with matching purple lip balm on fullish luscious lips. Alert, pretty, soulful, deep-brown Italian eyes. Large golden hoop earrings. *Very* large. Purple fingernails, and, I have little doubt, matching purple toenails. Tall, maybe five foot nine in bare feet, gym-trim, without a single extra pound, and bustier than you might expect. Wearing a hyper-tight black dress. I won't attempt to fathom the designer. With jet-black Spanx, with black skyscraper spikes that elevated her total height to at least six feet. Carrying a black briefcase.

Who wears spikes to a tort's exam?

No, she didn't look like a hooker with a briefcase. She looked perfectly lovely. She looked like a Jersey Girl.

Actually, an EJG.

Which is Luca's term, meaning Extreme Jersey Girl.

Which might seem both an illogicality and an impossibility, but it's not.

I looked at Miss Angela from the couch where I was reading old court transcripts.

The Papp case.

"Why not?" I asked, risking a smile.

"Because I only like 'tough guys' in movies."

Which we both knew was a lie. Jersey Girls *love* tough guys. Swat guys. Seals. Boxers. Etc. They also love guns, illegal tasers, and mace.

Maybe I should take a personal moment to address this "Jersey Girl business" which first popped up yesterday, momentarily, when the Boss was singing.

Let's face it, "Jersey Girls" are the most famous girls in America. If not the entire world. No one's ever heard of "Nebraska Girls" or "Dakota Girls," even though I'm sure they're all lovely. Yeah, we've heard of "California Girls," something I've had an up-close-and-personal experience with (she's currently playing volleyball on Hermosa Beach), and I've also heard about "Southern Girls," which, appealing as it sounds, seems pretty generic. But the term "Jersey Girls" is anything but. It's hyper-specific and universally known.

First, let me back up a minute. *All* the girls in New Jersey are marvelous, and not all of them fit into the standard definition of "Jersey Girl," but *all* of them, even my nerdy fed pal, have "Jersey Girl" within them.

OK, back to the "stereotype." I've described an example up above (thank you, Angela), but what else? What's beyond (or beneath) the big hair, the big makeup, and the showy clothes?

> *Put your makeup on, fix your hair up pretty*
> *And meet me tonight in Atlantic City.*

Springsteen again. ("Atlantic City.")

"Jersey Girls" are opinionated, independent, confident, and outspoken. Talky, tough, and resilient. Sometimes too loud. Sometimes too brash. But always good-looking, body-conscious, and clothes-conscious. They're deeply loyal, deeply honest. Often to a fault. Shopping is one of their non-gym cardios. Dancing is the other.

All Jersey Girls like to dance.

Categorically.

They wear T-shirts that say:

> *Yes, I'm a Jersey Girl.*
> *What are your two other wishes?*

They also love deeply, unconditionally.

Life-and-death, "forever" love.

Back to Springsteen again:

> *Nothing matters in this whole wide world*
> *When you're in love with a Jersey girl.*

Did I mention they talk a lot? Matt McCusker describes the melodious accent as "a mix of 'valley girl' with a splash of 'Rocky.'"

Meaning they speak like New Jersey.

He also says, going a bit too far, that their "gym outfits look a lot like stripper outfits."

Yes, they've got "cousins" across the Hudson in Brooklyn and parts of the Bronx and Manhattan. Marisa Tomei in *My Cousin Vinny* could easily pass for a Jersey Girl.

Enough of that. Maybe I've said too much already, but I couldn't resist. The appearance of Miss Angela Rossini has proven to be both distracting and thought-provoking.

To say the least.

"Have a seat," I said.

She didn't want to, but she knew that Savannah had hired me, so she parked her trim bottom on the low table in front of me.

A florid blast of perfume wafted over me, and I didn't mind at all.

I thought I'd be congenial.

"How'd the test go?"

"I'm smarter than I look."

I had no doubt.

She looked at me oddly, above the Ray-Bans.

"What's that thing on your head?"

Tact obviously wasn't her strong suit.

"It's what it looks like."

She was referencing the previously mentioned "cross" on my forehead, about an inch high, carved into my skin.

A scar.

She wouldn't let it go.

"How'd you get it?"

"Only my lovers get to know."

Which was not exactly true.

I'm hardly self-conscious about the thing. Actually, I'm not really self-conscious about anything. But it's proved to be extremely useful. It creeps people out, and it's definitely more effective as a "mystery."

So I tell no one.

"Then I guess I'll never know," Miss Wiseass responded.

"There's no guessing about it."

Despite her cocky bravado, she seemed momentarily hurt, even stunned, that I wasn't "interested."

It was time to get serious.

"Tell me about the judge."

She softened. Noticeably.

"He was a kind and brilliant man."

"Did he ever take you down to the basement?"

She got angry.

"Infuriated" might be a better word.

Did I mention that Jersey Girls get angry? Extremely angry. Especially EJGs. They're always talking about "kicking somebody's ass." Often males. But other females even more. Most commonly other EJGs. It can happen suddenly, anywhere, but most likely on a Friday or Saturday night. The later, the better. Usually someone from one gang of gal-pals disses somebody in another gang. An insult of some kind. A slight. Like Fortunato's slight of Montresor. Then the alpha of group A gets over-mouthy with the equally mouthy alpha of group B. The word "bitch" is tossed around ubiquitously, supplemented with emphatic "f-words," and even a few "c-words." Then, suddenly, the talk ends, and they glare at each other and square off.

As in some primordial ritual.

Which, I have to admit, is even more fascinating than those amazing Youtube square-offs from Australia between the extremely pissed-off kangaroos.

Or ostriches.

You can't take your eyes off it, and no one *ever* intervenes. I've broken up a ton of guy punch-outs over the years, but I'll never step in the midst of one of these.

Into what's coming next.

When one, or the other, with blazing speed, with the speed of light, attacks the other. Fortunately, it quickly devolves into a grunting and hair-pulling match (in which, of course, there's plenty of hair to get ahold of), with subsequent rolling around the boardwalk or down to the pavement, with scratching, gouging, and I'm obligated to report, occasional biting.

Suddenly it's over.

An invariable stalemate. Each of the alphas is immediately swarmed by their respective pals, who assure her that the other girl is either bleeding to death or already in an ambulance.

Eventually, in each group, a mirror appears from nowhere, as the pretty combatants stare at their respective reflections in the revelatory glass, at disheveled hair, smeared eye shadow, and squished lipstick. Not to mention a broken fingernail or two.

"I look like 's—.'"

Although guaranteed by all around her:

"You should see the other bitch."

(Or "ho.")

Angela gave me her alpha look.

"What does *that* mean?"

"The house has a basement. Were you ever down there?"

"I didn't even know it had a basement."

I believed her.

I gambled.

"How long have you been sleeping with the judge?"

She said nothing.

Then she dropped her pretty head and cried. Sobbed, in fact. The judge was obviously *much* more than just her mentor, and I felt sorry for her.

When she got control, she looked at me directly. Her eyes were wet, but her eye shadow was remarkably undisturbed.

"Don't tell Savannah."

It was much stronger than it reads on the page. She was begging.

"I won't unless I have to."

It was the best I could do.

"I'm after the man's murderer," I assured her, "not his love life."

She understood.

"Are you suspicious of anyone?" I asked. "Did he mention a problem with anyone?"

"Never. But I was just his intern, and I only met him for the first time a year ago."

She thought it over.

"Savannah once told me about a problem with some contractor guy named Greco, but I think it was over years ago."

"Did he ever mention András Papp?"

She seemed confused by the name.

"No. I've never heard of him."

I nodded.

"Can I go?"

"Yes."

She rose once again and walked across the lounge as if nothing had happened. As if she hadn't lost her lover. As if she wasn't afraid that her best friend would find out. As if she hadn't cried about the mess in her life.

I thought she was marvelous. Not really my type, but marvelous nonetheless.

Provided she hadn't killed anybody.

I put the transcripts aside and checked out Nonna's report on the Garvey family:

Judge Glenmore Garvey (age 55, Passaic County Judge):
Savannah Garvey (age 22, Rutgers Law Student)
Daniel Garvey (age 20, Princeton junior)

I'm sure you know more about the judge than me. The ubiquitous word seems to be "respect," with a whole bunch of "distinguisheds." Born in Harbor View, Jamaica, he came to Paterson with his parents when he was three. An only child, a definite overachiever, he went off to Rutgers, then law at Yale, and then met his wife Carita on a trip "home" to Kingston. They married the summer after he graduated law school, when he began clerking in Paterson under Judge Wilcox. Then he and his wife bought a home in Pines Lake in Wayne. He moved up fast, got a reputation for being "tough but fair," for never tolerating any nonsense in his courtroom. It was, apparently, the same at home. Carita raised the kids to be like their father, and their family life seems to have been both loving and encouraging as well as demanding.

Thirteen years ago, when the kids were ages nine and seven, Carita was killed in a boating accident on a trip back to Jamaica. On Montego Bay. The judge was crushed, and he never married again. As far as I can determine, he never even dated again. Despite the tragedy, he kept the kids on the path that Carita had set for them, even though he'd often say that he'd "spoiled them." But I've seen no signs of that.

Savannah, I'm sure you've noticed, is a beauty like her mother. After Princeton, she decided to go to Rutgers Law and stay close to home. Her mother raised her "proper," but not "superior" or "entitled." She seems to have a lot of friends, but not many boyfriends. None serious. Maybe she's wary of men. I'm sure she'll be wary of the likes of you.

Daniel, the younger brother, seems a lot like his sister, but a bit more self-conscious. He clearly likes expensive clothes and pretty girls, but he manages to keep his grades up and keep himself out of trouble. He's majoring in journalism, and he currently has a knock-out girlfriend at Princeton, Kimberly Watts, from Wykoff.

Neither the judge nor his kids have ever had any trouble with the law. They seem like an odd, likable, success-driven, loving trio.

Carita, whom I never met, would be proud.

She'd also be proud if the knucklehead I work for would figure out who hung her beloved husband from the living room ceiling.

Love, Nonna

Nonna always refers to her grandson (Luca) as a "knucklehead," and me as well, along with a string of other derogatives. Always with "love."

It was time to head south.

Within ten minutes I was heading down 21, heading for the Parkway, blasting you-know-who.

"Where the Bands Are":

> *And when I tell you that I love you,*
> *Tell you that I love you*
> *I wanna have to shout it out loud!*

12. Surf City

S HOULD I knock you around?"

I was standing in the living room of Sykes's little cottage in Surf City, about seven miles south of the Hathaway beach house.

The place was his primary address, but it didn't feel "lived in." It didn't feel like someone's home. Sykes was sitting on the couch in the throes of some kind of breakdown.

"I'm not big on patience," I lied.

Actually, I'm *very* patient. It's necessary in my racket, but I really didn't know what to do with the guy, which was the kind of frustration I've never cared for.

I got here a few minutes ago. Previously, I'd picked up Zoe at the beach house, then left her outside, up the block, so I could "pick at" Sykes alone. But there wasn't much to pick at.

He didn't even come to the door when I knocked. Fortunately, the door was open, and I found him inside holding his head and whimpering on the couch. Yeah, sure, the guy had lost his girlfriend, in a horrific murder, but I'd never seen anything like *this* before.

Gallagher had called him "barely coherent." I'd call him a clinical basket case.

Was it grief?

Was it guilt?

Or was it something else?

"Talk to me, Sykes."

He mumbled again.

Something like:

"Not here."

Which, of course, made no sense.

I grabbed him by the hair and forced his face upward. Toward mine. Yeah, I felt sorry for the guy, but I had a murder to figure out.

"What are you talking about, Sykes?"

He looked at me blankly. I had no confidence that he actually saw me.

"I'm not here. Not here. Gone. Dead."

Great. My primary suspect thought he wasn't "here."

I let him go.

I remember reading, years ago, about Cotard's. Was it possible? It's some kind of weird syndrome, a nutty delusion, where people become convinced that they're dead even though they're obviously not. It was first described by some French guy, some neurologist named Cotard, who described a "gestation" stage of the usual suspects: depression, despair, and self-loathing, which then, somehow, morphs into a sense of personal negation, a denial of one's self-existence. They stop eating, stop taking care of themselves, become essentially inactive, and withdraw from everything.

I know it all sounds like crap, but you can look it up. It's super rare, of course, and maybe Sykes is, quite simply, out of his mind with grief.

Or faking it.

I stepped back and looked at the guy. He was disheveled and pathetic, but he was also, underneath it all, a bit of a looker. I thought it over. In the cinematic vein. Maybe he looked a bit like Sam Shepard. The actor who wrote the boring plays, not the Ohio doctor, spelled "Sheppard," who got convicted of murdering his wife back in the fifties, did ten years in the can, got himself acquitted at a second trial, and ended up a professional wrestler.

Jessica Lange had fallen in love with the *Right Stuff* guy, and I could see how Chloe might have been attracted to this guy before he became a raving lunatic.

Should I call the hospital?

Or the cops?

I dialed Gallagher. He picked up.

"I'm with Sykes, and the guy needs help. He's totally out of his mind, probably suicidal, and he needs to be in a hospital flushed with antipsychotics. He can't even communicate."

"I'll get on it right away."

I liked Gallagher. No messing around.

I went over to the window and looked outside. The night was falling with twilight-gray. Up the street, I could see Zoe sitting on the hood of my XTS, thinking whatever she might be thinking. I didn't want her to see Sykes like this, so I sent a text saying I needed another ten minutes or so.

I watched her text back.

No problem, "Mr. Colt."

Wiseasses are everywhere.

I walked over to the far corner of the room and sat down in an old chair, ready to check Nonna's short text:

The guy who wrote the short story, which I still can't find, is Eduardo Williams, who seems to be a literary nobody. Not even a wiki page!

At least the grumpy librarian was working on it.

Then I read her report on the next-to-last girlfriend of the blithering idiot sitting across the room:

> *Camille Anderson (age 25, Wall Street type):*
>
> *I found Camille on something called Facebook (something you've probably never heard of). I'm not sure if she's Sykes's next-to-last girlfriend or his next-to-next-to-last. She and Sykes seem to have gone out briefly at the beginning of the year, in January and February. Her few references to Sykes seem pretty routine. She grew up in Alpine, extremely wealthy, an only child. She's also a smarty-pants. She went off to Wharton, then joined her old man's highly successful financial consulting firm, Anderson & Steele, on Liberty Street near the Federal Reserve. She commutes from her condo in Cliffside Park. No rap sheet. Private and clean.*
>
> *Ask her for some financial advice.*
>
> *Love, Nonna*

The hard-ass granny always pretends that I'm a financial moron. Actually, I make plenty of money, much more than I need, which the old goat knows since she's got access to all my financial records and accounts.

I looked at Sykes. His lips were moving but nothing was coming out. He wasn't drooling yet, but he looked catatonic. I didn't even try to bring him back to the real world.

It's stuff like this that makes you grateful to be whoever you are.

Then I heard it.

A distant sound. One I knew well. Too well.

A buzzing.

I stood up and stepped over to the window. Up the street, Zoe was slumped to the ground, having been tased, and a dark figure was standing over her with a knife.

Ready to use it.

I didn't have a clean shot.

At least not one that wouldn't jeopardize Zoe, so I pulled my Colt and fired through the picture window into the dark night sky.

Above them both.

Glass shattered all over Sykes's living room.

Up the street, the assailant was startled.

I ran to the front door, rushed across the lawn, then up the quiet street. Zoe was sitting on the pavement, and the dark figure was gone.

"Did you see anything?"

"No, he tased me from behind."

She was still stunned by the idea.

Off in the distance, on a parallel street, I heard a car race off. It was too late to pursue.

"Are you all right?" I asked.

Asking the question I should have asked first.

"Yeah."

Then she looked up at me directly, through her ridiculous glasses.

Dead serious.

"I want 'in' on this, Colt. All the way in."

"Fine," I said.

What else could I say?

II

There are more than 2,500 cemeteries in New Jersey. Be careful.

— Thomas C. Colt

13. Cliffside Park

Friday, May 13th
62°

H E DUMPED me."

She shrugged when she said it as if it didn't faze her in the least. Maybe it didn't.

I was sitting on her pristine all-white couch in her pristine all-white luxury condo in the Winston Towers on the Palisades in Cliffside Park. On the thirtieth floor. Overlooking the Hudson. Overlooking the George Washington Bridge. With a huge picture window facing yet another spectacular view of the New York City skyline.

She sat comfortably in a matching, white chair, facing her couch, facing me.

Everything in her apartment was expensive, except for me.

Winston Towers is one of three luxury high-rises built on the site of the old Palisades Park, once the most famous amusement park in America. (Along with Coney Island.) The place shut down in 1971, so its heyday was long before my time, but my uncle went there a lot when he was a kid, and he's told me lots of stories. The place, apparently, was magical. The Tunnel of Love, the famous

Cyclone, the Wild Mouse, and the world's largest saltwater pool. It was also famous for raucous rock-and-roll concerts with the likes of The Shirelles (Jersey girls from Passaic), The Chiffons, Leslie Gore (who grew up in Tenafly), Bobby Rydell, Fabian, Chubby Checker, Frankie Avalon, and then, later, Diana Ross, Michael Jackson, the Rascals, and the Lovin' Spoonful. Most important of all was Freddy Cannon, who had a number-three smash hit with his upbeat rock-and-roller "Palisades Park," about a guy who meets a girl at the park and falls in love in the Tunnel of Love:

> *You'll never know how great a kiss can feel*
> *When you stop at the top of a Ferris wheel*
> *When I fell in love down in Palisades Park!*

The place had an even longer history than my uncle could remember, way back to 1898, and it's actually mentioned, from across the river, by F. Scott Fitzgerald in his novel, *The Beautiful and the Damned*:

> *Across the water were the Palisades, crowned by the ugly framework*
> *of the amusement park—yet soon it would be dusk and those same*
> *iron cobwebs would be a glory against the heavens, an enchanted*
> *palace set over the smooth radiance of a tropical canal.*

At the moment, I was sitting in the enchanted palace of Camille Anderson, mid-twenties, a wealthy girl from wealthy Alpine, designated by *Forbes* as "the most expensive zip code in America," who was also, obviously, *very* smart. Smart enough to go to Wharton, the billionaire factory that once produced Walter Annenberg, Warren Buffet, Laurence Tisch, Donald Trump, Elon Musk, etc.

She was pretty too.

With short strawberry-blonde hair, almost pixie-like, explosive eyes (I'll come back to them in a minute), high cheekbones, fullish lips, careful makeup, and a personal-trainer body. Maybe looking a bit like Annie Lennox, but much prettier.

Wearing flats. Wearing a light-green dress. Wearing it like it was her gym outfit. Casual as hell. Confident as hell.

And those eyes.

Camille has Zoe's eyes. That weird golden shade of amber, which I looked up yesterday. It's very rare. *Extremely* rare. Maybe Bryan Sykes has a thing for yellowish-orange eyes, what some people call "cat eyes," what others call "wolf eyes."

It's, apparently, the result of an excess of some pigment called lipochrome. Unless you prefer to believe the jackass theory that it's the result of alien impregnation. Amber eyes, it seems, can be best accentuated, not that they need any accentuating by a light-green eye shadow.

Which Camille was wearing.

Given the rarity, there's plenty of mythologies floating around about people with amber eyes.

> *They're more beautiful.*
> *They're more spiritual.*
> *They're extraordinary lovers.*
> *They have psychic powers.*
> *They die young.*

I hope the last one is wrong.

"Actually," she continued, "he just stopped calling."

She didn't seem concerned about it.

"You don't seem upset."

She gave a shrug. It was a wealthy girl's shrug, which always adds a touch of superciliousness to a shrug's normal disinterest in the matter at hand.

"We only went out for a few months," she explained. "Besides, I'm happy with my new guy."

"Tell me about him."

Not meaning the new guy.

"He was polite, attentive, and a bit peculiar. But I liked him."

"Some people think he's a murderer."

"What? That's ridiculous!"

She was genuinely shocked, even a bit pissed.

At me.

"I thought you said there was a 'traffic accident.'"

"That was my lie to get in the front door and up to the thirtieth floor."

I wondered if she'd throw me out, but I had the odd feeling that she actually admired my deception. I wondered about her scruples. Or lack thereof. I wondered what she was doing with other people's money over on Wall Street.

She ignored my prevarication. She was still shocked that Bryan was involved in a homicide.

"What's it about?"

"His current girlfriend was murdered two days ago down at the Shore."

"Well, Bryan didn't do it. I can assure you of that. He's a very gentle soul. Actually, he's even a bit of a wimpy soul."

"He doesn't look it."

"Bryan wouldn't hurt anyone."

"Did you ever see him depressed?"

"No. Why?"

"Never?"

"Never."

"Why did you say he was a bit 'weird' a minute ago?"

"I said, 'peculiar.'"

I waited as she thought it over, wondering how to explain.

"Too fastidious, I guess. A bit obsessive."

"About what?"

"About me."

I believed her.

"What can you tell me about Chloe Hathaway?"

"Nothing. Is she the dead girl?"

"Yes."

"I've never heard of her before, and I haven't had any contact with Bryan since February when he stopped calling me."

Then she remembered something.

"She's not that girl at Barnegat Light?"

"Yeah."

"It popped on my phone the other day. A news alert. I had no idea that Bryan was involved."

She mulled it over.

"How horrible," she decided.

"Did he give you that ring?"

She was wearing a small silver ring on her left ring finger. It was simple, plain, maybe even cheapish. It didn't match anything else in the room.

"My niece gave it to me. Why?"

14. Cliffside Park

THE STIFF looked pretty good.

Actually, I'm a closed coffin/cremation kind of guy. Just put my dust (ashes) inside a little box inside the big box.

Thank you.

The judge was a distinguished-looking man who looked the same way in his coffin. His dress shirt collar covered the rope burns on his neck. Unfortunately, word had finally leaked out about the "prison cell" in the basement, and it cast yet another pall over the normal, wake pall.

I wondered if the judge had any last words, probably not.

But a lot of undeserving criminals got the opportunity to have *their* say, and some of my uncle's favorites flashed through my mind when I should have been paying my respects to the dead.

Who knows? Maybe the judge would have enjoyed them.

> *"The rest of the world can kiss my ass!"*—Johnny Frank Garrett, executed for the rape and murder of a seventy-six-year-old nun.

> *"Somebody needs to kill my trial attorney."*—George Harris, murderer, executed in 2000.

"You sons of bitches, give my love to my mother!"—"Two-Gun"
Crowley, sitting in the Sing Sing electric chair.

*"I wish the whole human race had one neck and I had my hands
around it."*—Carl Panzman, Mississippi mass murderer.

Lovely.

Fortunately, I was distracted from my distractions.

Savannah came over and kissed me on the cheek. She smelled
lovely, and she looked lovely. Dressed in black, sad as hell. I wished
I could do something about it, but I couldn't. On second thought,
maybe I could figure out who put her father in the box. Maybe *that*
would help.

I said something nice about her old man, something truthful,
and then I moved back into the crowd. It was an afternoon session,
but the place was packed. Packed with a "who's who" of Passaic
County law enforcement. Lawyers, cops, politicians, along with the
younger friends of the two kids. Off in the far corner, Angela was
sitting by herself, in another world, a world of loss and sorrow, so I
left her alone. Judge Mackenzie was there, of course, having surely
attended Meredith's wake last night in the same exact funeral parlor,
in the same exact room.

Unfortunately, Luca couldn't make it. He was planning to attend
the night viewing tonight.

I moseyed around, making people uncomfortable.

Talking to many.

Interrogating.

Then I spotted the kid, the son. Daniel. Sharply dressed.
Handsome. Preppy. Princetonish. Kind of perfect. Just like his sister.
He was standing with an equally striking young woman, surely his
girlfriend, surely Kimberly Watts, tastefully dressed, expensively

dressed, but not at all showy. A pretty blonde with hair tumbling down to her shoulders.

I walked over. Daniel seemed glad to see me.

"Mr. Colt."

We shook hands.

"This is my girlfriend, Kimberly."

We shook hands as well.

"Can we talk?" I asked.

"Sure, why not right now?"

He looked at his girlfriend, who clearly understood, and we walked out of the death room and found an empty, much smaller death room.

I didn't bother to ask where he was two nights ago since the Wayne cops had confirmed that he was down in his dorm room at Princeton working on a take-home exam.

"How are you holding up?"

He shrugged.

"I loved my old man, but this prison cell in the basement is really creepy. What's it all about?"

"I don't know yet."

"Would you tell me if you did?"

He spoke politely.

"Yes."

"I always thought my old man was a bit heavy on the law-and-order stuff, but I never took him for a hypocrite. Never. But what kind of judge imposes his own punishment? In his own basement!"

I didn't have an answer.

"Were you ever down there?"

Meaning the basement.

"No. I didn't even know it existed. When we were kids, my father added a new wing on the house, but I was never aware that it had a basement. Neither was Savannah. For obvious reasons, I guess. I'm told that one of the bookcases in his study covered the entrance."

"That's right."

"A lot of kids seem to grow up thinking that their old man is a fraud, or a hypocrite, or superficial in some way. I hear it all the time from other kids. But I've never felt that way until this morning."

He seemed like a serious young man.

Thoughtful.

Like his father.

"Let's see how things play out first."

That was the best I could do.

He nodded, dissatisfied.

It was time to talk about murder.

"Any idea who killed him?"

"None. Judge Mackenzie says it probably has to do with one of his trials, which certainly makes sense, but I never knew anyone who didn't like my old man."

"Nothing odd? Nothing suspicious?"

"Savannah once told me she thought he was being blackmailed."

"By whom?"

"She didn't know, and she later decided that she was wrong about it."

"Why?"

"I don't know. I was down at school."

"Anything else?"

"Not that I can think of, and believe me, I've been thinking a lot the past two days."

I understood.

"Maybe you should get back in there."

He nodded.

We reentered the crowded viewing room. He quickly found Kimberly, and together they joined Savannah near the coffin. I looked around. A room full of suspects. There were hundreds of them, coming and going.

I spotted Johnny Madero, and I sent him a text.

"Meet me in the lot."

I watched him check his phone then head for the door.

Outside in the parking lot, Madero was nervously lighting a cigarette. I think the guy's always nervous, but I've always made him even *more* nervous. Johnny was a well-known political operative in Paterson. Part Hispanic, part Italian, part sleazy fixer, part nerdy strategist. He was small, thin, fortyish, and I always thought he was rather stupid-looking. Unattractive. I won't bother to insult some actor by attempting a comparison.

Maybe I'm being too hard. The guy kept his record clean, and he was never out of work. He was exactly what he was. Sometimes he was very useful. Until a few weeks ago, he was Meredith's campaign manager.

Until he wasn't.

"Still pushing for cancer, Johnny?"

"Yeah, hard as ever."

As mentioned, I made the guy nervous. I make a lot of people nervous, and Madero had trouble looking me in the eye.

In the shades.

"Who killed the guy in the box?"

"How would I know something like that, Colt? But there's sure been a lot of talk about Cortez. The judge hit him pretty hard back in the sentencing phase, but then I heard he's got some kind of alibi."

"Yeah, he was with his girlfriend," I said sarcastically.

"Not exactly airtight."

"You got anything that can help me, Johnny?"

Off in the distance, I saw Kimberly weaving through the numerous parked cars, finding her blue Lexus. Then she was gone.

"If I did, you'd be the first to know. Even before the cops."

Oddly enough, I believed him.

"What about Meredith?" I threw out.

For the hell of it.

"I think it's pretty obvious, right?"

"Say it out loud."

"No one messes with the Ravellos."

"Why did you leave her campaign?"

"I couldn't take it anymore. The bitch was a super-bitch. You ought to know, Colt, didn't you date her a bit?"

It wasn't an accusation, but he regretted it as soon as he'd said it.

But I didn't take umbrage.

Hell, it was all over the news back then. It was even in the tabloids.

"Every man makes one mistake in his life."

"I've made billions," he assured me.

"Don't add to your list by not telling me something I need to know."

"I won't, Colt."

Once again, I believed him.

15. Wake II

THIS ONE looked a lot better.

Beautiful, in fact.

Which was never a term I'd associate with Zoe, even though they're identicals. "Cute," yeah. "Pretty," yeah. But not "beautiful."

Maybe it's the glasses.

Chloe's eyes were closed. Damaged underneath. Mutilated. Amber no more.

The evening viewing was crowded.

Zoe sat with her parents, all three looking crushed, doing their best to greet old high school friends, neighbors, Emerson friends, and a handful of Chloe's Random House colleagues.

I made the rounds.

I'm one of those people who upsets the balance in any room I walk into. Any crowd. It's not charisma, and it's certainly not some kind of allurement. It might have something to do with celebrity, I suppose, but it was going on long before I got my PI rep in the Pine Barrens case. It's simple. I make people uneasy. I'm big, I'm intimidating, and I'm even threatening when I'm not threatening.

The truth is, I really don't fit in anywhere, which is fine with me. When people are edgy, they tend to reveal things, and I tend to make people edgy.

I guess I'm blessed.

I roamed around the place, meeting with various suspects, attempting to be polite, asking them rude and inappropriate questions. Sometimes insulting questions. Like, "Where were you when Chloe was killed?" Stuff like that.

I should also admit that I like wakes. They gather the suspect pool. In unhappy unsettling circumstances. Then *I* show up. Like the grim reaper.

Even bigger.

I was doing the same thing earlier this afternoon at the judge's wake, but without much success. Unless you consider eliminating possible suspects as a success of some kind. Which it is. A kind of tedious progress.

So I made the rounds, searching for persons of interest, "persons of *my* interest," making a tragic affair even bleaker than it already was.

Yesterday, after disrupting the Paterson Chess Club, I drove into the city and paid a visit to the Random House Tower on Broad and Fifty-Sixth. Which is now known as the Penguin Random House Tower, due to the merger. The publishers of approximately twenty-five percent of the US book trade, Random takes up the first twenty-seven floors of the fifty-two-story building, which houses luxury apartments on the upper floors. Chloe worked on the fifteenth floor of the publishing giant, once founded by Bennett Cerf and jump-started by James Joyce's pretentiously boring *Ulysses* back in 1934. But they made up for it by publishing Faulkner, not that he sold many books until he won his Nobel.

I talked to some of Chloe's colleagues and friends down in the lobby, with its impressive floor-to-ceiling, glass-enclosed bookcases and the rest up on the fifteenth floor. All of whom seemed to "love her to death." An inappropriate way to describe it. But I spent most of my time in Manhattan sitting in the neat-as-hell small office of Raven Davenport, Chloe's immediate superior and closest work-buddy.

Thirty-two, friendly, plumpish, and pretty-faced, with appropriately raven hair. Who, it seems, is happily married, with two young kids, who loves working right where she's working.

Everything was "great."

Except that her best friend had been murdered and mutilated.

"No jealousies?"

"There's always plenty of that," she admitted. "Everywhere, right? Even at Random, but Chloe kept her distance. She avoided the gossip, and she avoided the backbiting."

I wasn't surprised. I assumed that Zoe was exactly the same way.

"You've got nothing?"

"Not really," she admitted, disappointed with herself, clearly wanting to help.

"What about her writers? They can be an irritating bunch."

She thought it over.

"I can't think of anyone."

"Think harder."

It sounded a bit aggressive, but she didn't seem to mind.

She thought harder.

"Actually, there was one jerk she had last year who was endlessly bitching that we weren't promoting his masterpiece enough."

"Blaming Chloe?"

"Blaming Chloe, but the guy lives in Amsterdam."

He sounded worthless.

"Give me his name anyway."

She wrote it on a sticky note.

"And the title of his masterpiece."

Which she did, then she handed me the little piece of paper.

I looked at the picture of her kids on the desk. A boy and a girl.

"Did your daughter give Chloe a little ring? A small silver ring?"

The question seemed to come out of left field.

"No," she said, rather surprised. "I'm sure I would have known. She's only five years old."

I satiated her curiosity.

"Chloe was wearing one when she died."

She went sad. In a flash. I was afraid she was ready to start crying, so I switched the subject.

"What about Sykes?"

"Is that Bryan's name?"

"Yes. Did you ever meet the guy?"

"No, but she talked about him all the time, especially in the beginning. She fell hard for Bryan, and I don't think that kind of thing had ever happened to her before. But things started tapering off."

"In a normal way?"

"I guess so."

Which is a pretty useless response in a murder investigation.

"Were there problems?"

"Not really, but I think the flame was burning out. Or at least burning a lot lower. The guy never seemed to work. Maybe he's loaded, but Chloe didn't know what to make of it. She also told me he was a bit obsessive."

"About her?"

"About her."

"Controlling?"

She thought it over.

"I wouldn't go that far. It just seemed to Chloe that Bryan's whole life was *her*, which started making her uneasy."

"Was she planning to break things off?"

"I don't think so. Maybe I'm exaggerating. Most of the time, she was telling me how thoughtful he was. How kind. Always trying to please her. What girl doesn't want some of that?"

"Unless it goes too far."

She nodded, thoughtfully.

"There *was* something else. Something that really creeped me out, which I forgot to tell the Barnegat detective."

I liked Gallagher, but maybe he was *too* polite.

"Tell me."

"Bryan told Chloe that one of his ex-girlfriends had been murdered. He was quite upset by it, and she tried to comfort him."

"When?"

"I think it happened in March."

"Where?"

"In New Jersey somewhere."

"Do you know her name?"

"No. That's all I know. Chloe mentioned it in passing one time, as something sad that had happened in Bryan's life, but it didn't seem to upset her at all. But I have to admit, it spooked the hell out of me."

"Did you tell her?"

"No. Maybe I should have."

It was self-questioning time.

Since I liked her, I tried to help.

"Maybe it has nothing to do with anything. Just forget about it."

She seemed appreciative.

"Where were you when Chloe was killed?"

She didn't seem insulted.

"At home with my loving husband."

That conversation was yesterday at Random House.

My cell zinged. In Barnegat. It was a text from Vinny Ravello, the don's oldest:

> *The don says, keep up the good work.*

I laughed.

Then I realized that I was standing in the middle of a wake. So I circulated some more, insulting people as I went, working the room.

Did I mention that the main suspect was absent?

Maybe that's perfectly obvious.

The boyfriend had spent the night in the psych ward at AtlantiCare Regional down in Atlantic City, and as far as I knew, he was still locked in his cage.

Trying to figure out if he was dead or alive.

Also missing, oddly enough, was Sykes's "best friend," maybe his *only* friend, Krish Singh, the neurologist at Hackensack Med.

So I talked to Raven again (nothing new), and Gallagher again (nothing new), and Special Agent Mark Eliot (nothing new), who'd been assigned to Zoe after last night's attack in Surf City.

I like boy scouts, even when they're thirty-six years old and working for the FBI. Just because I'm a compendium of rough edges doesn't mean that I can't appreciate a good-guy fed who's married to his job. Attractive, unattached, likable, a bit "Ken-ish." Meaning the doll. Wearing a blue fed suit.

What else?

Mark Eliot was "all about" the job, the assignment, and I had no doubt that he'd do everything he could to protect his fellow agent. He'd spent last night in the room next to Zoe's at Sand Castle Bed & Breakfast on Bayview Avenue in Barnegat Light. It's a nice-looking bayfront inn, a boutique of sorts, with a grand piano in the parlor, a library, and a rooftop deck with great views of the bay and the lighthouse.

"Keep her off the deck," I told him last night.

"I will," he assured me, and I believed him.

"Why isn't she packing?" I asked him tonight, a bit irritated.

"She decided against it. After all, it's her sister's wake. Do you really think some guy's going to walk into the funeral parlor and start shooting?"

"I've seen worse, and I bet you have, too."

He thought it over, keeping his eyes locked on Zoe, sitting next to her parents, next to the coffin.

"You're right," he decided.

I let it go.

"What do you make of the parents?"

"What you see is what you get. Nice people, great parents from everything Zoe's told me. Completely devastated."

When the visitor line at the coffin came to an end, Zoe stood up and walked across the room.

To me.

Eliot gave us space.

"Where's your piece?" I said, realizing that I should have said something about the dead. Expressing my sympathies.

Which I definitely had within my heart, but if anything happened to the pretty girl standing in front of me, there'd have been a lot more sympathy making the rounds.

"It's good to see you, too," she sarcasticized.

"Take off your glasses."

"Is this part of the case?"

"Yes."

She took them off. Her golden eyes glittered at me directly.

She was equally as beautiful as the girl in the coffin.

She put them back on.

"Why don't you wear contacts?"

"I like looking the way I look."

It wasn't defiant; it was matter-of-fact.

"I like it too. You look lovely."

Which I'm sure I shouldn't have said. For a long list of reasons.

Her ambers suddenly flushed with wet, and she leaned into me and held me tight. Everyone noticed, pretending not to notice. I felt her gently shudder with a few soft sobs. Then it was over.

She let me go, then looked at me again.

"I'm sorry."

She attempted to explain.

"I've lost a part of myself."

I grew up an only child, but I imagine losing a sibling must be horrible, and losing a twin must be horrendous, but losing an identical must be absolutely incomprehensible.

Like losing oneself.

"I better get back to my sister."

I nodded.

"I'm staying down the Shore tonight," I explained. "Here's the number. Eliot has it too."

I handed her my office card with a black silhouette of a Colt Python on the front and my phone number handwritten on the back.

"I don't sleep much," I said. "Call me anytime."

"I will."

"I'll see you in the morning."

Meaning the funeral, the burial, etc.

She nodded gratefully.

"Thanks, Jack."

I watched her walking back across the room to the dead body of her best friend, her sister, her twin, her other self, and I wanted, more than anything, to protect her from evil.

My cell pinged, so I went outside into the cool night air of the Jersey Shore.

It was grandma from hell.

"How's the prettiest grandmother in the United States?"

"Doing more work than you, I'm sure."

She wasn't really angry, but she never missed a chance to let me know how hard she was working.

Which I've never doubted.

"Any results?"

"Of course."

She made me wait.

"You'll have your 'Reparation' tomorrow."

She explained.

"Eduardo Williams first published the story eleven years ago in some obscure literary journal called the *Gloaming Zone*. (I'm sure Rod Serling is rolling over in his grave.) The *Zone* only lasted a few issues, and none of them are posted on the web, but Williams included the story in a collection that came out last year from a small press in Arkansas. It's his one and only book, which Amazon is overnighting, which is called *One-and-Twenty Tales*. Which I guess is a pretty lame reference to *Twice-Told Tales*."

"Anything on Williams?"

"Not much, except that he's dead. There's only a few fragments about the guy on the web, and no one bothered to review his book. From what I can tell, he grew up somewhere in Maryland, went to USC undergrad, then published a few inconsequential poems and stories. He spent his later years as an expat in Portugal, in some place called Coimbra, where he married a Portuguese girl."

"When did he die?"

"Last year, on a flight back to Lisbon from the States. He died in his seat. Maybe some kind of heart thing."

"How old was he?"

"Fifty."

"I wonder if 'someone' could track down the widow's phone number?"

She laughed and hung up.

I stood alone in the dark night of the early summer. Within the comforting breeze. I could smell the ocean. Even this close to the house of death, nothing compares to the nights and darks of the New Jersey Shore.

16. Tequila

Friday, May 15th
48°

A GUY WALKS into a bar.

But this is no joke.

He's jacked on coke and tequila, he's packing a .38, and he's looking for someone. Actually, he's looking for money.

He's on the lam. For several reasons. Parole busting, aggravated assault, and the primary suspect in a triple murder in Pines Lake.

The Wayne cops are looking for the guy. So are the Paterson cops. So are the State Troopers.

Two hours ago, Cortez walked into his cousin's apartment in the Fourth Ward and said, "Give me that .38."

Meaning an old Smith & Wesson, snub-nose, Model 36, J-Frame.

His cousin, a tough guy with his own extensive rap sheet, wanted no part of Carlos's troubles.

"Sure, Carlos. Whatever you want."

Domenico's is a not-unfriendly dive bar on Lafayette Street, near Wrigley Park in Paterson. Not far from the old Lafayette Bar and Grill at the corner of Eighteenth Street, where Rubin "Hurricane" Carter, one-time middleweight contender, and John Artis shot up the place back in June 1966. Long before my time. Three people ended up dead. Carter and Artis were convicted at two separate trials. Then Hollywood made a bogus movie about Carter called *Hurricane*, which portrayed him as innocent, which everyone in Paterson knows is a lie.

Cortez walks into the bar.

There are good guys in this world, and there are bad guys, and there are guys like Cortez. Psychos on the verge of exploding at any given moment. Over anything. Over nothing. Whenever they walk in a bar, or anywhere for that matter, everyone in the room gets edgy and looks the other way.

Cortez sees what he's looking for.

Miss Ruby Johnson.

A harmless, seventy-year-old African American woman. A regular at Domenico's, with a drinking problem.

Gin Rickeys, always with two lime slices.

Ruby's sitting where she always sits, in the far-back, left-side table in the saloon, facing the bar.

Three months ago, she hit the lottery.

Some said it was thirty thousand; some said it was fifty thousand.

Actually, it was five thousand, and it's long gone. For back rent, for credit card debt, for her granddaughter's car payments, for Gin Rickeys.

Cortez spotted her and walked to the back of Domenico's.

Nearby, chained to the bar, was Poison, the owner's pit bull, over sixty pounds, watching everything with seeming disinterest.

It seems he's developed a fondness for the old lady.

Cortez didn't waste any time.

"I need cash."

Which seemed almost humorous to Ruby, but, fortunately, she didn't laugh.

"It's all gone, sonny boy."

"Give me that purse."

It's still unclear what Cortez was planning to do if there was no money in the purse. Which, of course, seemed highly likely. Would Miss Ruby actually walk around this part of town at night with anything much in her purse? Maybe Cortez planned to take the woman back to her apartment so he could search for the cash. Maybe he planned to take her to the nearest ATM.

So he could get the hell out of town.

It's uncertain.

She clutched at her purse.

"No."

Poison stood up.

Apparently, Cortez doesn't like dogs, especially pits. I have to admit I'm not a fan myself. According to the CDC, the breed kills about twenty-five Americans each year, one every sixteen days, mostly women. Typically, they're hold-and-shake maulings. Unfortunately, the dogs have become a status symbol for various gang bosses and drug dealers.

As for dogs in general, I'm fine with them as long as they don't bark. You might say, "Well, that's ridiculous, that's what dogs do!" but babies cry all the time, and we train them not to, and many considerate dog owners do the same. Every time a dog is sold in America, the new owner should be handed a copy of *Barklessness* by Bill Edward Web. It's a training manual. In his famous essay "On Noise," Schopenhauer claimed that the worst sound in the world, the most "thought disrupting" sound, was the crack of a cart driver's whip. Maybe he was right back in 1851, but these days, I'd have to say it's barking dogs.

I suppose I've just alienated forty-four percent of my audience, but I wish them (and their four-leggeds) well.

Honestly.

Since honesty's always the best policy.

One of the unique traits of the pit is that, before it strikes, it seldom glares, bares its teeth, or growls.

It just strikes.

Which happened late Friday night at Dominico's.

Poison lunged, snapped his chain, and went directly for Cortez's neck. But he missed, getting hold of the man's left shoulder.

I'm guessing that Cortez is impressively pain-tolerant because all the witnesses claim that he didn't make a sound, and he certainly didn't seem to panic. He pulled out his snub-nose, jammed it beneath the pit's jaw, and blew a .38 up through Poison's head, into the ceiling.

Then he tossed the dead dog down to the floor, and he looked down at his money ticket.

But Miss Ruby was working on her fifth sparkling Rickey, and she did what she definitely shouldn't have done.

She laughed.

Cortez shot her in the face, calmly grabbed her purse, and headed toward the front door. On the way out, he spotted the owner, Miguel Domenico, standing behind the bar.

The owner of the bar, who was also the owner of Poison.

Domenico turned and tried to run away.

Cortez shot him in the back.

Twice.

Ruby died instantly. Miguel died six hours later in the emergency room.

Calm as could be, Cortez walked outside, into the Paterson night, clutching the woman's purse, containing $37.53, leaving behind a million witnesses.

17. Cemetery

A SHES TO ashes, etc.

The priest was wrapping things up.

Around the coffin, it was mostly the same group as late last night at the wake, but everyone looked even more catatonic. The word "grief-stricken" makes a lot of sense. Everyone looked like they'd been pummeled with the heartbreaking loss of Chloe Hathaway. They weren't just suffering from grief. They'd been stricken by it.

As things wound down, the crowd dissipated, moving slowly toward their various cars.

Since there's no cemetery on Long Beach Island, the Hathaways were burying their beloved Chloe at St. Mary's on Beachview Avenue in nearby Manahawkin.

I have to admit, I like cemeteries, and this one was exceptionally beautiful, not that that helped the mourners very much.

Then I saw him coming.

From another direction.

Sykes had somehow escaped his cage, and he was now heading for the coffin. Fortunately, the crowd was mostly gone. He looked like a man on a mission, and I could see the bulge beneath his windbreaker. At his belt. I met him at the grave.

"Give me the gun, Sykes."

He knew I was ready and willing to take it.

He said nothing. He just stared at the grave and handed me his Beretta. A newish APX Centurion.

The safety was on.

"Do you know where you are, Sykes?"

He ignored me, still focused on the coffin that was waiting to be lowered into the grave.

A shot rang out.

Off to my right.

Over by the few remaining cars.

I looked over as Mark Eliot collapsed to the ground right next to the family's funeral limo. Fortunately, Zoe's parents were already in the backseat, but Zoe was standing next to Eliot.

Above him.

A second shot rang out as I rushed through the tombstones. The assassin was firing from a moving black SUV, maybe a Ford Expedition, with tinted dark windows, that was moving quickly past the black limousine.

Zoe was hit.

She fell to her knees, then grabbed Eliot's Glock. Which I later learned was a 26. She immediately fired off eight rounds at the fleeing Expedition. By the time I got there, she was already assisting Eliot and calling 911.

"Look at me, Zoe!" I called out.

She turned, and I could see that she was hit in the left shoulder. Not too bad.

I was proud of her. Miss big-glasses, desk-office FBI agent had handled things as well as anyone.

Her terrified parents started coming out of the limo.

I looked at the car parked behind it, waiting at the curb. It was an Acura RLX, hunter green, with some old high school friend of the twins sitting in the driver's seat, clearly astonished by what he'd just seen happen right in front of him. I considered pulling the kid out of his car and chasing the SUV, but it was too far gone.

Damn!

Then I remembered something.

I looked back at the gravesite. Sykes was gone.

Damn!

But I had an idea where he might be going.

And why.

I opened the door of the Acura and pulled the kid out on street. Then I hopped inside and fired up the engine.

Instantly, the door on the passenger side opened, and Zoe got inside.

"Get out, you idiot! Wait for the ambulance."

"Not a chance."

Fine.

She was pressing at her shoulder with a scarf or something, and she seemed to have the bleeding under control.

I burned out.

"Did we just steal Eddie's car?" she said.

She seemed to be enjoying herself.

"Shut up and press."

She laughed.

18. Old Barney

Friday, May 14th
58°

THE LIGHTHOUSE again.

I raced up Long Beach Island, up Central Avenue, in my "recently appropriated" hunter-green Acura, screeching into Barnegat State Park. I could see Sykes off in the distance, sitting in front of the entrance.

"He's sitting in the same position!" Zoe said loudly.

I drove as close as I could get, then slammed on the brakes. I thought I could see a glint in the sun.

A blade.

As I got out of the car, I pulled my Python and fired several times into the air, into the ocean, hoping to distract him, as I rushed toward the lighthouse.

"Sykes!" I called out.

To no effect.

Then I stopped where I was and shot him in the right shoulder, but he didn't seem to notice. He casually switched the blade to his left hand, then drove the point upward, powerfully, beneath his chin, deep into the center of his head.

Like Chloe.

The blood gushed downward over his shirt. Into his lap. Then his head slumped forward. He was dead before I got there. I called 911, asking for two EMT trucks.

One for Zoe, who was now standing beside me, clutching at her wounded shoulder, and one was for the pathetic creature slumped in front of us.

It was hard to make sense of anything that was happening.

"What's going on, Colt?"

I didn't bother to answer her question.

I turned, looking at her hard.

No nonsense.

"You're going to New York, and you're going to vanish until this thing is over."

Meaning some kind of FBI safe house.

She didn't bother to argue.

I could tell she wanted to, but she didn't.

19. Eastside Park

I SUPPOSE I was in a bad mood.

Some people think I'm always in a bad mood, but I'm not. Almost never. But maybe this afternoon I really was in an angry mood. An uncompromising mood. Even listening to the Boss on the long drive to Paterson didn't help that much.

After all, my "client" had been tased and attacked last night. Then she'd been shot today.

Maybe my uncle was right:

Only an idiot takes two cases at the same time.

After the lighthouse, we went directly to AtlantiCare Regional in Atlantic City, where they patched her up, and I waited for her new protective agents to arrive from New York City. A male and a female eventually showed up, both looking determined and highly competent. As for Zoe's previous babysitter, he'd been struck in the stomach, which perforated his liver and some other stuff. The surgeons had operated right away, and he was now off the critical list. Still unconscious, but doing OK.

"Was it Bryan?" she asked.

Meaning, was it Sykes who shot her and Eliot in the cemetery?

"No."

"Are you sure?"

"Yes. He didn't have enough time, and I took his Beretta at the gravesite. Besides, the black Expedition wasn't at the lighthouse, but Gallagher found an abandoned rental, which he traced back to Sykes."

She was confused.

She wasn't the only one.

"What's next?"

"You let the feds hide you away somewhere, so I can keep working."

"What about your other case?"

"I'm heading north as soon as they escort you out of here."

She understood.

"Be safe, Colt," she said, and she touched my arm gently. It was a gesture of concern, a sign of endearment.

Zoe style.

I was now cruising through Eastside Park, east of downtown Paterson, over sixty acres of parkland near the Passaic River in the Third Ward. Which is full of historic homes, actually mansions, where the Paterson elite used to live back in the days when the city was an industrial powerhouse. Eventually, the area went "bad," falling into shabbiness and disrepair, until the "gentrification" began. Now the place is trying to recapture some of its old glory.

I pulled in front of a handsome Tudor, where a construction crew, Greco Construction, was laying the foundation for a sizable addition.

I parked behind one of the cement trucks and walked over to the guy who was obviously in charge.

Joey G. Greco, probably mid-forties, was a tough-guy contractor who'd built the extension on Judge Garvey's house thirteen years ago. Meaning that he'd also built the concealed basement and, most probably, the prison cell, even though he told the Wayne cops the basement was "empty."

Nothing inside.

The year after the extension was finished, Greco filed a lawsuit against the judge alleging inadequate payment. For some reason, the judge settled out of court two years later, but there was definitely bad blood between them, even though Greco made light of it, telling the Wayne cops, "Hell, that was years ago. Water over the bridge."

He sensed me coming.

People usually do.

He's about five foot nine, sturdy-looking, a bit squattish. His head is also a bit squattish.

He looked up from his clipboard, and he definitely wasn't pleased. He certainly wasn't about to roll out the welcome mat.

"I know who you are, Colt, and you can get back in your slick-black Cadillac and go back wherever you came from."

As mentioned earlier, I was in a bit of a bad mood.

I shoved the guy hard, backward, down into a large low catch-basin full of wet cement. Immediately, Greco's "big boy" came over to protect his boss. "Avenge" his boss. The guy was even bigger than me. Maybe six foot four and over-muscled. To show everyone, to "show himself off," he wore a Guns N' Roses wifebeater T-shirt. Too bad I never cared for GNR. Too bad I never cared for "gym" muscles. What serious athletes call "show" muscles. "Beach" muscles. The end result of a much too popular kind of gym-ratting that's done entirely for narcissistic reasons, not to enhance one's athletic prowess, not to heighten one's athletic competitiveness.

Don't get me wrong. I do my own gym diligence. I've got an intimate relationship with a certain heavy bag at Ike & Randy's boxing gym on Park Avenue in Paterson, but it's all for professional enhancement.

Professional readiness.

This moron's goal in life was to walk down the boardwalk at Seaside Heights on Saturday night and show off his show-off muscles.

You get the point.

I wasn't impressed.

He came at me without hesitation, grunting a sentence fragment peppered with expletives. Nevertheless, I didn't come here to hurt the guy. Or anyone else. If he were smart, which I felt certain he wasn't, he'd know better than to get too close. To touch me. To lay a hand on me.

That's the trip wire.

Sure enough, he went to grab me with both hands.

I wondered what I should do with him. Sure, I could simply incapacitate the guy. Momentarily. But I didn't care for his attitude. I've always hated bullies.

So I decided to break his ribs.

Actually, "fracture" his ribs.

As he went to grab me, I hit him with a left hook right below his "gym" pecs. I could hear them crack. Before he buckled, tumbling to the ground in a heap, his eyes blew up with pain, nearly popping out of his head. Then he lay helpless in the grass, struggling to breathe.

I showed my usual compassion.

"Breathe slowly and don't get up."

I wondered if I should tell him about the world of pain he had waiting for him. Cracked ribs are a bitch. I should know. I got popped with the helmet of a Syracuse running back in my sophomore year at Rutgers, and I was out of action, *any* kind of action, for at least six weeks. Fortunately, the Syracuse game was the last game of the season.

I decided against it.

Why not let him learn the hard way. His goon-pals at the gym won't be seeing him for a while.

I looked at the other guys in Greco's crew who were still standing behind the squirming big boy. Guys who, a few minutes ago, would have gladly kicked the crap out of me. Now they weren't so sure.

"Go back to work," I said.

They did.

Then I turned to the moron lying in the wet cement, who was starting to sit up in the slop.

"Stay there."

I said it firmly.

He stayed there.

"I want to know what you *didn't* tell the cops."

He understood, and he waited for my questions.

"Who designed the extension?"

"He did. The judge. He drew out some sketches. He knew exactly what he wanted."

"The concealed basement?"

"Exactly. He was big on that. He even sent the kids away until we were finished, then he made me sign a nondisclosure."

"About the jail cell?"

"About all of it."

"You put the bars in, right?"

He hesitated.

Then he looked over at his wheezing big boy.

"Yeah, but I had no idea what I was doing, so I Googled some stuff and did exactly what he wanted."

"Did he explain why?"

"No, he just called it a 'novelty.' So I never questioned it. Rich people are weird; they want all kinds of wacko stuff. So what if a judge wants a jail cell in his basement? I figured the guy was eccentric. Maybe he was planning to have some parties down there."

The guy was a load of it.

"You put *people* in jail cells."

He didn't deny it.

"Look, the guy paid me, and I didn't ask any questions. I never thought he was going to imprison someone down there for thirteen years."

Which was probably true.

"What was the lawsuit *really* about?"

He shrugged.

"Just to bust his balls."

"About what?"

"I'd asked him for a favor. After all, I was keeping his 'secret' a secret, right? So I figured he owed me."

"What favor?"

"My stupid-ass nephew got a DUI, so I asked the judge to make it go away. I didn't demand anything, I just asked him to help me out, but he dismissed me. Like it was absurd. Like I was insulting the guy."

"What happened?"

"We came to an understanding."

"Tell me."

"I dropped the suit, and I promised to honor our NDA. I also promised not to ask him for any more favors. Basically, the judge gave me eight thousand dollars to go away and shut my mouth. Which I did."

I said nothing. I let him stew in his goop.

"That's everything, Colt. Everything! I promise."

I tended to believe him.

"Did you ever blackmail the judge?"

He looked at me like I was crazy.

"Who'd be stupid enough to blackmail a judge?"

"Maybe someone who was stupid enough to file a lawsuit against a judge."

"Not blackmail, Colt! No way."

I continued my train of thought.

"Maybe someone stupid enough to be sitting in wet cement."

20. Brownstone

A s mentioned, wakes are like Agatha Christie's roundups, but post-burial receptions are even better.

Probably the booze.

Tonight, the Garvey reception was being held in the Grand Ballroom at the Brownstone. The same place where Meredith learned the final tally on her "foregone conclusion" mayoral race. Where she was subsequently murdered right outside. Right afterward. Where her own post-burial reception had been held last night.

I'm sure that many of the same people were back tonight. The Paterson elite. Without the governor. Without the First Lady.

I roamed around a bit, making people uncomfortable everywhere I went. People will generally greet me pleasantly, even though they're really hoping I'll move my ass along. I talked to Savannah briefly, then Daniel, then Matthew Harker, the judge's long-time legal assistant, who was still walking around in shock four days after the murder.

Probably sixty or so, Harker had never married. He lived alone in a condo in Riverdale, not far from the judge's home in Pines Lake. Like the kids, he assured the Wayne cops that he'd never known anything about a basement, let alone a jail cell, and the very idea of his boss doing something unethical, something illegal, seemed to invalidate everything that Harker had done with his whole life, which he'd totally dedicated to the judge. To the judge's notions of legal justice.

I hit the guy with a few indelicate questions, but he was worthless, so I let him float off into the room like a lost and abandoned child.

Then I pestered a bunch of other people, but mostly I kept my eyes open, watching everyone, watching their interactions.

Getting nowhere.

Eventually, I took a seat in a long row of chairs on the perimeter, next to my best friend, Luca Salerno, chief investigator for the Passaic County Courthouse.

We've known each other since we were kids, since we went to school together, since we played a lot of hard-hitting linebacker together.

We talked briefly about his kids, the Mets, and murder.

Cortez's girlfriend had finally caved, so the thug's alibi for the Garvey killings was toast.

Eight years ago, Judge Glen Garvey sent Carlos Cortez to Rahway State Prison for attempted murder. The jury didn't believe his lawyer's song-and-dance about "self-defense." The fact that Cortez's victim, whom he'd almost beaten to death with a beer bottle, was a decorated war vet, with a family with young children, didn't help much either. Cortez was a well-known Paterson lowlife, with an extensive rap sheet, mostly violent stuff. The judge had had enough. He sent him off to Rahway. But Cortez, always a hothead, lost his cool several times during the trial, threatening both the prosecutor and the judge. At sentencing, he threatened to come back and kill Judge Garvey.

The trial was a local sensation, and after Cortez got out, after doing eight of his twenty, he was heard by several witnesses "sounding off" about the judge in a string of trashy Paterson bars.

Then the judge was shot-and-hung in his living room.

Then Cortez went berserk at Domenico's last night.

"We picked him up this morning," Luca said. "Down by the river."

"Anything useful?"

"Yeah, we found a coil of rope in his van. The same kind."

Meaning the same kind as the kind wrapped around the judge's neck.

"Of course, he denies it's his."

"Of course."

"You like him for it, Luc?"

"No. Do you?"

"No."

Vincent Ravello walked by in a billion-dollar suit, nodding respectfully in my direction. I guess he was here representing the don. Maybe even checking up on me.

"I hate that bastard," Luca said.

Loudly.

Luca and Vinny have hated each other ever since we were little kids. Their multitudinous fights were always titanic affairs, bloody affairs, and they always ended in a draw of one kind or another. Someday one of them will kill the other one. I guess it's up to me to make sure that Luca comes out the other side.

"Anything else?" I said, distracting Luca from his bête noire.

"Angela's DNA is all over the place. All over the house, the living room, and the judge."

"They were lovers."

Luca was surprised.

"You sure?"

"Yeah, I told her I'd keep it a secret. If possible."

"Isn't she best friends with the daughter?"

"Exactly."

He understood.

"Are the Wayne cops pressing her as a suspect?"

"I don't think so. She was over at the house quite a bit, and she interned for the judge. DNA makes sense."

"Good."

I changed the subject.

"What about Meredith's ballistics?"

"I thought you weren't interested."

"I'm not."

He laughed.

"My guy says the shooter used Winchester cartridges. Expeditions. 142 grain."

"Four fires, four hits," I said.

"Yeah," he agreed.

"It's interesting that the bodyguards were wounded, but you-know-who was shot to kill."

"That's true."

He thought it over.

My cell pinged.

"Take it," he said. "I need a drink."

He stood up.

"Keep away from Vinnie."

"Yeah, sure."

He vanished into the crowd, and I answered my phone.

"Colt."

It was Xander Demetrios, my super-hacker kid who does the stuff that Nonna wouldn't do. Meaning the illegal stuff. The *really* illegal stuff. I like the kid a lot, who's actually twenty-five, and I pay him well. I also like the fact that, like me, he doesn't believe in wasting time.

"The money goes to the Innocence Project."

Meaning the blackmail money.

I was surprised.

"How much?"

"Twenty thousand dollars every month."

"Any idea who's doing it? Who's been blackmailing the judge?"

"No idea."

I switched things.

"What about Papp?"

I was referring to Lukacs Papp, the brother of the man I found dead in the judge's prison cell. The brother was coming from Budapest to claim his brother's body.

"He's flying into Newark tonight. British Air 104. 10:38 p.m."

"Good work, Xander."

"Anytime, Mr. Colt."

"One more thing."

He waited.

"A guy named Bryan Sykes offed himself this morning at Barnegat Light. His home address is Surf City. I want to know who gets his money."

"I'll figure it out."

I knew he would.

As I hung up, I noticed that Savannah was talking with her brother. They didn't seem very happy with each other, so I got up and walked over.

"What's going on?"

"Sister and brother stuff," Savannah said with a shrug.

Daniel, however, wasn't in a shrugging mood. He looked at me directly.

"Did you see the obituary she wrote?"

"I did."

"Maybe a bit too much? A bit over the top? The guy incarcerated a prisoner in his secret basement, and Savannah makes him sound like Mother Theresa."

He had a point.

He seemed as much conflicted as angry.

His sister offered no defense.

Neither did I.

"Maybe you shouldn't blame your sister for loving her father."

It was pretty weak, and I knew it, but it was the best I could come up with.

It worked. Somewhat.

"I loved him, too," he said. He looked at his sister. "All right, the bloody hell with it."

Then he walked away, probably looking for his pretty Kimberly.

"He's having trouble with everything," Savannah said, in a sisterly kind of way. "So am I."

"You're doing great," I assured her.

She looked into my shades.

"Thanks, Colt."

Which made me feel like crap since I hadn't solved this mess by now.

Resolved it somehow.

My cell phone pinged again, and she was distracted by several friends who clearly wanted to "outdo" the obituary.

It was Nonna.

I found the dead girl.

Good. Things were starting to happen.

It pinged again.

The book's in your mailbox.

I texted back:

Did you find a phone number for the widow?

She responded:

Yes, my lord and master.

I laughed.

Soon the place started emptying out, so I went outside to the empty alley. I couldn't resist the temptation. Which was *especially* irritating since Pamela Hopkins had said, arrogant as hell, that I'd be unable to resist. I pushed her out of my mind and looked around the place where her daughter, Meredith, the mayor-elect, had been assassinated by Winchester cartridges. Luca had told me enough about the case that I knew the approximate trajectories. I looked over at a three-story rooftop where the shooter had lain in wait.

In the darkness.

I heard a noise, which didn't feel like a threatening noise. I turned around. It was Savannah, looking lovely in the Paterson moonlight, looking worn-out, looking weary.

"Take me to your place, Colt."

It sounded like a bad idea.

"It sounds like a bad idea."

"I don't care."

We walked to the mostly empty parking lot, and I held the door open, and she got inside my XTS, and we drove up Garrett Mountain to Stone House.

In silence.

Inside my living room, she sat on my couch. Actually, she collapsed *into* my couch.

Then she broke the silence.

"I'd like a drink."

"I don't have much. Whiskey or brandy."

"I'll try the brandy."

I went to my kitchen and poured her a small glass. When I got back to the living room, I handed her the glass.

"Why so small?" she kidded. "Is it a thousand dollars an ounce?"

I'd already smelled the wine on her breath, which was lovely, by the way. Did I mention that she was beautiful?

"I don't get women drunk on my couch."

She smiled.

"I doubt that, Colt."

She took a sip. A long one.

"Sit next to me and hold my hand."

I sat next to her, but I didn't hold her hand.

But I did look into her eyes. Deep, dark, Jamaican. And her lovely face. Her skin was flawless. How does a white guy attempt to describe such a thing without getting himself into trouble? Let's just stick with "beautiful."

Maybe "perfect."

She leaned over and kissed me. She tasted like brandy. She tasted marvelous. She tasted like the definition of temptation.

"This is the wrong time and place," I assured her.

She smiled again.

Well, at least, she was smiling.

"It's what the shrinks call 'transference,'" I said, not really believing it.

"What a load of crap!" she laughed. "And you know it, Jack Colt. We were made for each other!"

I laughed as well.

"You can spend the night in my bedroom. It's the one with the antique rifles on the wall."

"Naturally. Who designed the place? Daniel Boone?"

I liked her sense of humor, and I liked her, but I'm not about to mess around with a girl four days after she found her father hanging from the living room ceiling.

I tried to shift the mood.

"Can you be serious for a moment?"

"I can try."

"You once told your brother that you thought your old man was being blackmailed."

"It was a foolish suspicion."

"It wasn't. He's been paying out twenty thousand dollars a month."

She put her brandy glass down on the lamp table.

"To whom?"

"To the Innocence Project."

"What? That's where Angela works!"

She was stunned.

"I don't know who was blackmailing him, but I don't think it was Angela."

She thought it over.

Romance had left the building.

"Are you sure?"

"No. Do *you* have any other suspicions?"

"No."

"Do you have any idea *why* he was being blackmailed?"

"No," she shrugged, "but maybe somebody knew about the man in the basement.

"Maybe."

She thought things over.

"I've got to go out for a while," I said.

She laughed again.

"You're trying to get rid of me."

"Not true."

"Where are you going?"

"My uncle's injured himself, and I need to bring him some pizza."

"It sounds like a grammar school excuse."

"It's true."

"I never took you for Florence Nightingale."

"I have many facets."

She stood up.

"I'm retiring to the Daniel Boone bedroom. You can discuss your impotency with your uncle."

"Instead, I'll tell him that I was a perfect gentleman."

She laughed again, and then she left the room.

I didn't want her to go.

Who would?

21. Stone Tower

I SENSE A *"turn" coming.*

Yeah. Got that right.

Let's keep things moving.

It seems that everything was as "good" as a childhood can get. At least a childhood where the boy had lost his mother and the girl had never known her father. But they had each other, and they each had one exceptionally good parent.

Then everything went south.

It happened when the kids were fifteen, in the month of August, when Edward Sykes accompanied young Tory to a Girl Scout "leadership" conference at Mohawk Lake. On the third and final morning, they woke up sick, both of them with severe respiratory problems, and they were rushed to the hospital. Newton Medical Center. It serves Sussex and several other rural counties. You know it?

Yes.

They'd contracted Legionnaires' disease.

I didn't know it was still around.

It's rare, but there are occasional outbreaks.

How'd they get it?

No one knows, and no one knows why that particular strain was so virulent. None of the other girls or any of their parents came down with anything.

It's like hyper-bad pneumonia, right?

Right, and there's no vaccine, and about ten percent die. The doctors did their best, flushing them both with antibiotics, and they waited.

Which one died?

Both. Edward went first, with his son at his side. Then two days later, Tory died, with Bryan at *her* bedside. Tory's mother was temporarily out of the room, and the young girl whispered something to her soul mate, and the doctor called TOD at 11:58 p.m. on August 29.

What did she whisper?

That's what I've been trying to figure out. One of several things, in fact.

You're a lousy storyteller.

You're like a child. You have no patience.

The wizened old man, laying out flat on his back in his disheveled cot, momentarily reexamined himself. A priestly thing to do.

You're right.

Shall I continue?

You shall.

He emphasized the "shall" sarcastically, but I let it go.

So the kid's naturally devastated. So is Debbie Blake.

Do you think the mother believed that she and Edward would eventually marry?

I don't know, but I wouldn't be surprised. I really don't know.
Maybe it was platonic.

There's not much of that running around these days.

Should I continue?

Proceed.

There was that "tone" again.

That's the problem with Jesuits. Even the good ones.

What?

The tone.

What tone?

The know-it-all tone.

*Look who's talking. I'm over a hundred years old and you're
barely thirty.*

You're exaggerating in both directions. You're ninety-eight,
and I'm thirty-two.

Same thing.

I continued without permission.

So the two of them, the boy and the woman, with half their
world swept away, inexplicably extinguished, managed to survive
the dual wake, the dual funeral, and the dual burial.

*Don't tell me the mother's going to start sleeping with the young
boy.*

He rolled his eyes.

I ignored his interruption.

At the gravesite, in light rain, the mother said something to
the boy that he didn't fully understand, but they were interrupted
by other mourners.

Let me guess: you're not going to tell me what she said.

How do you know that *I* know?

It wouldn't be much of a story if you didn't know the key
plot points.

I ignored him again.

The next morning, Bryan rises early, eager to ask Debbie Blake what she meant at the gravesite. He dresses, eats breakfast, and goes next door. He knocks twice and goes inside, just like he always does. But he finds Debbie sitting in the living room, in her favorite chair, with a book in her lap.

Dead?

Dead.

Of what?

It's never determined.

Did they do an autopsy?

Yes.

Do people die like that? Of no apparent cause?

It happens. Don't ask me to explain it.

How old was she?

Thirty-five.

It's hard to believe.

A lot of this is hard to believe.

Now the boy's all alone.

Yes. Two days later, a local lawyer informs Bryan that Mrs. Blake had changed her will on the morning of the day before she died, right after the burial, and she left everything to Bryan.

Am I supposed to believe that she "willed" herself to die?

Yes. It happens.

It's hard to believe.

There's more.

He waited.

She had over sixteen million in the bank. She was apparently the daughter and heiress of a pharmaceutical CEO, but she always kept it a secret because she never trusted her husband.

Even before she married him?

Yes.

Was the girl illegitimate?

Probably.

Did she ever tell Edward Sykes?

I don't know, but I don't think so.

So now the kid's a millionaire.

Many times over.

Who decades later ends up with a dead girlfriend, a dead ex-girlfriend, and a knife shoved upward into his head. Self-inflicted.

Yes.

It's a pretty creepy story. Even with the missing parts.

It's not over.

Of course it's not.

22. Morgue

M Y CELL pinged.
Loudly.

It was early in the morning, much too early for me, but it was a text I was waiting for:

The Hungarian's here.

I dressed quickly, grabbed my copy of the short-story book, and drove straight to the Passaic County Morgue.

The Hungarian was already in the icebox, staring down at the corpse of his dead brother. Except for the "dead/alive" factor, they looked a lot alike. Small, thin, wiry. Rather ordinary looking, early fifties.

I let him mourn.

When he was done, he signed some papers for the ME as an attendant attended to the body, which Lukacs would be flying back to Budapest tomorrow morning.

When I approached him, he was willing to talk, so we found

an isolated, empty room. His Hungarian accent was thick, but his English was clear, and I liked the guy. As Nonna had already informed me, he was some kind of textile merchant who came to New York several times a year to close out business deals. As Xander had already informed me, he'd been in the city on the night his brother was shot to death.

I didn't waste time.

"You were here when it happened."

"Yes, in Manhattan. I took care of some business then flew back on Wednesday."

"Were you with anyone that night?"

Meaning, do you have an alibi?

Which he understood.

"Not in the evening. I was staying at the Marriott Marquis on Broadway alone in my room."

No alibi.

"Did you have any contact with András during the trip?"

"No."

"Before the trip?"

"Just a few letters over the years."

"From where?"

"Ossining. Or, at least, András *believed* he was in Ossining. From the beginning, he asked me not to visit. Begged me, in fact. He told me that he was content with his life, with his memory of his wife, with his books. That he was making 'restitution.'"

"In solitary confinement?"

"Yes."

"I tried to change his mind over the years, hoping he'd let me visit, but he said he preferred his solitude. So I respected his wishes."

"Are you sure it was your brother who wrote those letters?"

"Yes, it was his handwriting."

"No doubt?"

"No doubt."

"Tell me about András. What kind of man was he?"

It clearly pleased Lukacs to recollect his brother.

"He was a man of the highest integrity. It's that simple, Mr. Colt. He was a good man, a religious man, and he wanted to be a family man. All of which might seem rather ordinary, but I believe my older brother was a man of exceptional character. I'm definitely biased, but I believe that anybody who'd ever met him would say the same thing."

It was quite an obituary.

"You have no idea why he was in Judge Garvey's basement?"

"None. Who's ever heard of such a thing?"

"You once sent the judge a nasty letter."

He didn't duck it.

"I did. I was very disappointed and very angry. I attended every day of the trial, and I thought the man put up a 'nothing' defense. Terribly weak. I know very little about your legal system, but it seemed like my brother was abandoned. Betrayed."

"Did András feel that way?"

"Not at all," he admitted, "which I found impossible to believe. He actually thought the judge was a "man of principle." He even thought the man was his "friend." Which I never understood. Even more so now."

Then it suddenly came to me.

At *that* exact moment.

Was it possible?

Have I been looking at everything upside down?

Was it possible?

I asked the Hungarian a few more questions then offered my sympathies.

He was grateful.

"Will you discover the truth?" he wondered.

"Yes."

Maybe I already had.

Or, at least, part of it.

I gave him my card and told him to call me if he needed me.

Then he walked away, a little man with a huge burden.

I felt sorry for him.

Wondering if I could alleviate his burden.

23. Garrett Mountain

Sunday, May 15th
56°

I WENT IMMEDIATELY to my car, sat in the driver's seat, and read "The Reparation."

Stunned! To say the least!

The story's backstory was exactly the same as the Papp case. With the names changed:

> *András Papp was Lajos Pehm.*
> *Judge Garvey was Judge Mitchell Carlyle.*
> *Kevin Keldon (who killed Papp's wife) was Carl Carter.*
> *Alex Fontaine (Keldon's lawyer) was Karl Lorraine*
> *Etc.*

But the resolution was different, *very* different, and very different from *El secreto de sus ojos*.

"Benign."

But there was a curious oddity in the Papp/Pehm backstory. One of the names remained the same.

Andrew Morris, the dishonest appeals court judge, now deceased, who'd thrown out Papp's conviction for political reasons, had exactly the same name in the short story.

Which could hardly be a coincidence.

The story's author, Eduardo Williams, clearly knew the pertinent facts of the Papp case. So the question was, of course:

> *Was his resolution of the case fiction?*
> *Or fact?*

Was his explanation for the prison cell in the basement somehow accurate?

True to life?

I felt confident that I knew the answer, but I wanted to be certain.

I also briefly wondered, being a film buff, if the story had influenced *El secreto de sus ojos*?

> The Papp case was 2003.
> The short story was first published in 2005.
> *El secreto de sus ojos* was released in 2009.

Was it possible that Juan José Campanella, who was directing episodes of *House* in California, had stumbled onto a copy of *The Gloaming Zone*, then started reworking the idea inside his head?

Setting the story in his native Argentina?

With a far less "benign" conclusion?

Who knows?

But I doubt it.

I pushed it out of my mind.

It was irrelevant.

I called Matthew Harker.

Then I called Coimbra, Portugal.

It was late afternoon in the ancient capital, and Joana Santos Williams was more than willing to talk about her deceased husband. A man "never recognized for his talents." They'd met at the University of Coimbra, where Eduardo was teaching a class on Borges. The widow's Portuguesed English was lovely, and we talked for nearly an hour.

When we were done, I drove to Stone House.

My house.

Harker was waiting on the front lawn.

Holding the book.

I parked my car and walked across the lawn.

The man looked edgy.

"I'm not going inside."

He was adamant.

"Why not?"

I had no idea.

"Because I'm afraid of you, Colt."

OK, I guess I should appreciate any man who openly admits his fears.

"I know the judge respected you," he explained, "but you make me nervous."

"Don't believe everything you hear."

It wasn't much consolation.

He held out the book as a peace offering.

It was a copy of *One-and-Twenty Tales*.

Earlier, when I called him from the morgue, I asked him to stop at the house in Pines Lake and look for the book in the judge's bookshelves. The house was no longer a crime scene, and he'd obviously found the book.

"What is it?" he wondered.

I ignored him and turned to the title page and read the handwritten note:

For my friend Glenmore, in the hope that he'll enjoy a few of the twenty-one, especially the one he inspired at the Amira Hotel. Blessings to you and your family.

It was signed:

Eddie W.

Eduardo Williams.

I looked at Harker.

"Have you ever seen this book before?"

"Never. What is it?"

Again, I ignored his question.

"Was the judge ever in Istanbul?"

Which came out of left field.

Harker thought it over.

"Yes."

"When?"

He remembered.

"August 2004."

"Why was he there?"

"A close friend from Yale was getting married in Istanbul. A native Turk."

"Did he ever mention meeting a guy named Eduardo Williams?"

"No."

I shifted things.

"I bet, over the years, you and the judge discussed many legal hypotheticals."

"Of course, many times."

"Did you ever discuss 'justice' in the abstract?"

"I'm not sure what you mean."

I wasn't exactly sure either, or how to express what I was trying to get at.

"Some kind of 'higher' justice?" I tried.

"Judge Garvey was definitely a religious man, and he certainly believed in a higher and more categorical justice."

"No, I mean an 'earthly' higher justice. Like when the legal system fails."

He thought about it.

"He did ask me my opinion a few times about something called 'subsequent' justice. About one's moral obligations to reparate the failures of the court system."

"Was he ever specific about it?"

"Never, it was mostly legal gibberish. The number of angels on the head of a pin. That kind of stuff."

"Maybe it *wasn't* so abstract."

Harker was a smart man.

"Is that why Papp was down in the basement? Some kind of 'subsequent' justice?"

The front door of Stone House opened, and something beautiful stepped outside. Barefoot. Her jet-black hair was wildly messed and seductively wild. She was wearing nothing but a huge, red Rutgers sweatshirt. The one I wear around the house. Surely with panties underneath.

She also wore a pretty smile.

"What are you two doing?"

Harker was shocked.

I tried to assure him.

"It's not what you think."

"That's right, Harker. Mr. Erectile Dysfunction doesn't find me attractive enough."

I laughed.

Harker was horrified.

"Somebody's definitely the prettiest girl in Paterson this morning. Come back in a few months, and maybe we'll start over."

She laughed, and I looked at Harker.

"I better take care of this. I'll call you later and tell you what I haven't told you."

He seemed reasonably satisfied.

I walked over to my open doorway and its lovely gatekeeper.

"We need to talk."

"Just what every girl wants to hear."

She crushed my heart.

So did the hyper-cute federal agent with the dumb glasses. What was the matter with me?

When Harker admitted his fears, I thought to myself, "Good for him, admitting the truth, but, as for me, I don't have any fears."

Yeah, people might find that hard to believe, but there's nothing that I'm afraid of.

Which I know sounds terribly arrogant, terribly cocky, but it felt like the truth at the time. But now, I suddenly realized that I *do* have a fear. A fear of falling. A fear of falling for every single pretty girl in the "pretty girl" state of New Jersey.

Then I followed the one wearing my red RU shirt into Stone House, my house, where she sat on my couch.

"You want to throw on some pants?" I suggested.

"I'm good."

I walked over to my "entertainment center," a bookcase full of DVDs, and pulled out two films. Then I went back to the couch and sat down.

Next to Savannah.

"I have some good news. Some of it's still supposition, but I feel very confident overall. It's a complicated story, Savannah, which, in essence, exonerates your father."

Suddenly, she was *very* serious, very eager.

"I'm not positive who killed your father yet, but I believe I know why he had a jail cell in his basement."

She waited patiently.

"He did it because Papp wanted it."

She was visibly excited.

"Tell me everything!"

"You already know the particulars of the Papp case, right?"

"Right."

"After Papp shot Fontaine," I explained, "he fired his defense attorney and asked to see your father. Which was very peculiar. Especially since your father had absolutely *no* defense experience. In 2003, your father had just finished his internship with Judge Wilcox. It was also a few months after your mother died. Maybe the man who'd just lost his own wife felt compassion for the Hungarian immigrant who'd lost his wife to a street thug, then shot the lawyer responsible for the mugger being 'loose' on the streets."

"Harker once told me," she remembered, "that everyone was shocked when my father agreed to meet with Papp, and even more shocked when he decided to take the case."

"Exactly. So *what* happened in that meeting? I know this sounds weird, but I think András Papp convinced your old man that he "deserved" to be punished. That he'd taken a gun and shot a man, and that he was a "danger to society." So he asked your father, a well-known man of integrity, to defend him in court and intentionally lose the case."

"What!"

"Your father not only lost the case, but he temporarily damaged his reputation by offering such a weak defense in the courtroom. Many people felt that his performance at the trial was "unconscionable." Even "shameful." But Papp got exactly what he wanted. A max sentence."

"How could you know any of this, Colt? It was a private meeting, and the two men in the room are dead."

"Because there's an account. Of sorts."

She was stunned.

Naturally.

"Where?"

"In some obscure short story."

"That sounds nuts, Colt."

"It is."

"Tell me."

"In August 2004, your father went to Istanbul to attend the wedding of one of his friends at Yale. A Turkish native who was getting married. He stayed at the Hotel Amira, and late one night he met another American over drinks on the hotel's rooftop. The other guy was a wannabe writer named Eduardo Williams, a recent grad from USC, who was in Istanbul to begin a solo tour of the Bosporus, Gallipoli, Troy, and Ephesus, then over to Patmos, Rhodes, and finally Athens for the Olympics. He had tickets for several events, mostly boxing.

"Anyway, your dad and Williams became drinking pals that night, swapping stories. It seems that Williams idolized Poe and Borges and Rod Serling, and he was writing a series of short-short stories, 'tales,' as he called them, all a bit on the odd side. I know for a fact that he told your dad the plots of two of his recently completed tales that night, one about a forger and the other about a so-called idiot savant."

"How do you know this stuff, Colt?"

"Because I talked to Williams's widow about an hour ago. She lives in Coimbra, Portugal."

"Could this get any weirder?"

I shrugged.

"I'll let you be the judge."

Irony unintended.

I continued.

"I'm sure you can see what's coming. Your father told Williams an interesting story about a judge who decided to gratify a man's desire for retribution by building a prison cell in his basement and allowing the man propitiation. Atonement. Penance. Williams was obviously intrigued, and he asked your father if he could change the names and fictionalize the story. Your father agreed. Maybe it was really the booze that agreed. I have no idea."

I handed Savannah her father's copy of *One-and-Twenty Tales.*

She looked at it.

Stupefied.

"Harker found this in your father's bookcase," I explained. "The story is called 'The Reparation,' and it begins on page nine. There's also a dedication to your father on the title page."

Savannah opened the book and read the dedication.

She was stupefied. Did I already use that word?

I tried to clarify.

"He must have sent your father a copy from Portugal last year when the book was published."

She looked at me directly.

"Is the story accurate to the facts?"

"Mostly. All the names have been changed, except for one, Andrew Morris, the slimy appeals judge who threw out Papp's conviction."

"That can't be coincidental."

"No, it can't, but I've got no idea if it was intentional or not. Maybe Williams lost track of his name changes, or maybe he and your father agreed it might be an appropriate, although obscure, indictment of Judge Morris."

"Who's now dead."

"Who's now dead, who was the man who made it necessary for your father, a man of integrity, to honor the wishes of András Papp, another man of integrity."

"How does the story end?"

"The judge, named Judge Mitchell Carlyle, is dying, and he tells the whole fantastic story to his astonished young protégé. Then he asks the younger man to take his place as the caretaker for Pehm, who believes he's in Sing Sing. In solitary confinement. 'Pehm' is the story-name for András Papp, who's become one of the judge's closest friends."

"Does he agree?"

"Yes, despite the obvious risk to his legal career. Later, after the judge dies, the young man, just like his mentor, becomes a close friend of the incarcerated Pehm."

Savannah stared at the book in her hands.

"I should add," I continued, "that in the short story, Lajos Pehm knows that he can leave *anytime* he wishes, but he prefers to stay where he is and make "reparation." I believe that it was the same for Andreas Papp. The man in your basement."

She nodded thoughtfully.

"It's a lot to take in, Colt, but I can't tell you how happy you've made me. Maybe my father shouldn't have done what he did, but at least he did it with high intentions. To help a good man reparate his sins."

"Exactly."

I held up the first DVD.

El secreto de sus ojos.

"Do you know this film?"

"No. Is it Spanish?"

"Argentinian."

I held up the other one.

Secret in Their Eyes.

"What about this one?"

She looked it over.

"No, but I like Julia Roberts."

She looked at me.

"Why?"

"I'll explain some other time. It's not really relevant."

She accepted it.

She already had enough to process.

Then I wrecked the mood.

"I want you to go to Jamaica."

"What?"

"Someone killed your father, and I think you're in danger. I want you out of New Jersey. Far away. And I want you to tell absolutely *no one* where you're going. Not even your roommate."

"Is it that bad, Jack?"

"I don't want to take any chances."

She decided immediately.

"All right."

"Put on some clothes and make your reservation. Then I'll

drive you over to the Brownstone, and you can get in your car and drive straight to Newark airport. *No* going home. *No* going to your condo. *No* contacting anybody but me."

"You're a tough character, Jack Colt."

"Good."

"Would you run away if I kissed you?"

"No."

I didn't.

24. Morristown

VALLEY FORGE was tough. Morristown was worse. Much worse.

Washington spent the two worst winters of the war in New Jersey, in Morristown, strategically placed between New York City and Philadelphia, protected by the Watchung Mountains. The second winter, the "Hard Winter" of 1779–1780, was spent in Jockey Hollow, during one of the coldest winters on record. At least twenty-eight snowfalls fell on the encampment that winter, with falls up to four feet high. Somehow, Washington's ill-equipped, close-to-starving army of approximately 10,000 survived the endless blizzards, the high snowdrifts, and the frigid temperatures.

Years later, Washington called it the greatest "extremity" of the war. Which says a lot, especially given the disaster at Kips Bay.

I drove through Morristown, the one-time military capital of the Revolution, listening, incongruously, to Bruce Springsteen. When I pulled in front of the house, he was singing "Hungry Heart," and I couldn't turn it off.

Everybody needs a place to rest,
Everybody wants to have a home.

Exactly.

When I first heard the song years ago, I assumed the title was a reference to Augustine's famous phrase about the pilgrim soul's "hungry heart." Which my Ignatian uncle once informed me comes from Augustine's "Commentary on the Gospel of John," which he encouraged me to read. Which I did. But I later learned that the song's title is actually taken from a line in Tennyson's blank verse masterpiece, "Ulysses":

For always roaming with a hungry heart

It was nice to think of a New Jersey rocker sitting around reading Tennyson.

Lay down your money and you play your part
Everybody's got a hungry heart.

No doubt.

I shut him off, then read over Nonna's report on Wendy Newman, Sykes's ex-girlfriend, who, like Chloe, ended up dead:

Wendy Newman (deceased, age 25, pediatric nurse):
After she was murdered, there were lots of nice tributes on Facebook and the funeral parlor's website. Yes, I realize that once you're "gone," people tend to emphasize the best and gloss over the worst. But this kid sounds like she was very special. Kind, dedicated to children, dedicated to her profession, and very popular. She also looks quite attractive in the pictures on the web. She went to Rutgers Nursing in Newark, then got a job at Morristown Med, where her mother works. Who's also a nurse, also pediatrics. It seems

*that the mother and daughter were very close, and Wendy
was still living with her mom in Morristown when she was
murdered in the hospital parking lot. The investigation
seems to be going nowhere. The lead detective is a guy
named Teddy Lanier, age fifty-two.*

Yeah, Sykes was a "person of interest."

*Oddly enough, Wendy has the same birth date as
Chloe Hathaway. What are the odds?*

You be especially gentle with the mom, Mr. tough guy.

Love, Nonna

I could see the mom from my car. She was working in a small
flower bed on the side of the house, an attractive but modest ranch.
She was probably trying to distract her mind from her daughter's
murder two months ago. Unfortunately, I was here to undistract her.

Earlier, I spoke to Lanier on the phone.

He was willing to talk, but he didn't have much to say.

Wendy had left the hospital around 2:00 a.m., heading toward
her car across the dark parking lot. From seemingly nowhere, she
took two 9 × 19 mm Parabellums to the head and died immediately,
falling to the ground. She was eventually discovered around 3:15
a.m. The only surveillance camera that picked up the shooting was
far away, and the assailant, concealed behind a large SUV, couldn't
be seen, then slipped off into the darkness.

"Was she stabbed?"

"No."

"Was her forehead marked?"

"No."

"Were her eyes mutilated?"

"No."

"Who do you think did it?"

"I don't have a clue. We looked at the ex-boyfriend, of course,

but it went nowhere. I'm at a dead end, Colt, and I feel bad for
Mrs. Newman."

Me too, but it was time to agitate old memories.

I walked over to her little garden. She was squatting next to
some pretty, red flowers that I'm incapable of identifying. She was
wearing a light-yellow sundress, shades, and a Mets baseball cap.

She looked up.

Since I'd called her earlier, she knew I was coming.

"Colt?"

When she stood up, we walked around the back of the house
to the outdoor deck, and we sat in the deck chairs.

"You want some iced tea?"

"You need it more than me."

The sweat was running down her face. It was the pretty face
of a forty-eight-year-old nurse who'd lost her daughter and wasn't
happy about it.

Who was weary, worn-out, probably bitter.

There was no sense small talking.

I'm no good at it anyway.

"Tell me about Sykes."

"I think he killed my daughter."

She wasn't beating around the bush.

"Any evidence?"

"No."

"Tell me, what was he like?"

"Very polite. Very attentive to Wendy, but I thought
something was off right from the beginning. Something phony.
I had the feeling he was up to something."

"What?"

"I have no idea."

She was getting angry but trying not to.

"Then he dumped her."

"Any reason?"

"Nothing I ever knew."

"Did Wendy know why?"

"I don't think so. She was totally shocked. It came out of nowhere."

"Was that the end of Sykes?"

"No, the bastard wanted something back. Something he'd given her."

"What?"

"A little ring. A piece of junk, actually, but he wanted it back."

"Did she give it to him?"

"Yes, she mailed it to Culver's Lake."

Which is where Sykes lived as a kid.

"Do you have the address?"

"I'm sure I can find it."

"Did Wendy ever go to Culver's Lake?"

"No, and she never saw him again after he dumped her with an email."

"What did it say?"

"Nothing much. Just a few lines. The usual crap about how wonderful she was, but how he didn't think things were 'working out.' That he wished her the 'best.'"

She looked at me in the warming May sun.

"The 'best,'" she repeated, with nothing less than a mother's hate.

Who could blame her?

"Did Wendy have enemies? Any issues with anyone? Anyone who was jealous of her?"

"No. I'm sure you'll think I'm 'motherizing' the memory of my daughter, but she was loved by everyone. You can ask anyone in Morristown."

I believed her.

"Sykes did it," she repeated. "Who else?"

"Did you tell the cops?"

"Yes. Lanier's a decent guy, but he hasn't got a clue."

She looked at me with what I assume is a "mother's gaze."

"I know who you are, John Colt."

I wasn't sure how to respond.

"I'm certain that you can find out who killed my baby."

"It's possible, but I'm overloaded with cases right now."

"I'll pay you whatever you want. I'll give you the damned house."

She meant it.

"Give me a couple of weeks, then we can talk again. I'd like to help if I can. But I'll also want your car along with the house."

She smiled. For the first time. It was lovely to see her smile. I bet she did a lot of that before her daughter was gunned down in a dark parking lot.

I went to my car and called Nonna.

She picked up.

"The Colt Agency. Murderers beware."

I've known Nonna my whole life, but I still never know whether to laugh or not. Whether it'll only encourage her.

"Could somebody check Camille's birth date?"

"'Somebody' was already planning to do that."

Of course, she was.

"By the way," she continued, "did you hear that Cortez confessed?"

"I don't buy it."

"Me neither."

I bet Luca didn't either.

25. Hackensack Med

Y OU HINDU?"
Maybe it was a stupid question, or at least a rude one.
Maybe not.

"Yes."

"Did you guys talk about it much?"

"Sometimes."

The guy's name was Krish Singh, and I'd read Nonna's report in the hospital lobby before we met in his office:

> *Dr. Krish Singh (age 38, neurosurgeon):*
> *Born in Surat, west India, he grew up in Red Bank since the age of ten. As you know, he was Sykes's roommate at Rutgers, and he seems to have been Sykes's only "real" friend. They kept in touch over the years, and Singh was planning to go to Barnegat Light this week to meet Chloe Hathaway.*
> *After Rutgers Med in Newark, he did two postdocs at NYU. He's unmarried, no children, and legally clean. He's also a neurological big shot at Hackensack, but from what I can tell, he seems to wear it lightly.*

*Sorry I don't have that much. His web trail is essentially
all medical stuff.
Love, Nonna*

"You believe in moksha, karma, and the liberation from saṃsāra?"

Maybe it sounded dismissive.

"Yes, half the world does."

He didn't seem mad, just a bit defensive.

He was a little man in an overlarge white medical coat, with intense brown eyes and dark brown glasses. He was also one of the top surgeons at the most prestigious hospital in New Jersey. Rutgers-affiliated Hackensack Med. The fourth-largest hospital in the country, with over nine thousand employees, and, among other things, the Audrey Hepburn Children's House for abused kids.

"What was Sykes's interest?"

"Bryan was interested in everything. He was a 'seeker.' A 'searcher.'"

"For what?"

He shrugged.

"Some kind of understanding, I guess. Like all of us, right? Some kind of apprehension of the truth."

"Anything in particular?"

"Not that I can think of."

He thought about it, then continued.

"You're aware that he was a double-major in psychology and religion, right?"

"Right."

I took a left turn.

"Ever see any signs of Cotard's?"

He looked at me like I was an idiot, yet somehow he did it politely.

"Of course not!"

"He was acting very peculiar at the end. Denying that he existed."

"I never saw anything like that."

"Why weren't you at Chloe's wake?"

"I wanted to, but I had emergency surgery early the next morning. Which is why I missed the funeral. I felt terrible about it, but I had no choice."

"What about depression?"

"Never. Nothing out of the ordinary for a young college kid. The truth be told, Bryan seemed very happy with his life. As if he had a purpose."

"What purpose?"

He shrugged again.

"His studies, I guess."

"What about women?"

"A few here, a few there. Bryan was an exceptionally good-looking guy, but he wasn't girl crazy like so many other undergrads. But women seemed to like him. To be honest, sometimes I was jealous of his natural ease with women, but none of his relationships ever lasted very long."

He looked at me intently.

"I'm sure you know that he lost his childhood girlfriend."

"Tell me about it."

"He met her on High Point Mountain when they were kids, and they fell in love. Instantly. Soulmate stuff. Then she contracted Legionnaires' when she was fifteen and died a few days later. Needless to say, he was crushed."

"Did he talk about her much?"

"Yes, quite a bit."

"Was he obsessed?"

He wondered how he should answer the question.

"Maybe he was, at least part of the time, but he was also pressing ahead with his life. As I mentioned, he seemed generally content most of the time. He was a great roommate."

"What did he tell you about the girl?"

"Mostly just normal boy-girl stuff. With some odd stuff as well."

"Try me."

"All right. He once told me about this weird hypnotism 'thing' that happened to Tory two years before he met her. When she was eleven. She went to a county fair in Sussex with her mother, planning to see some hypnotist perform. When the mother volunteered, she convinced her daughter to volunteer as well. So the guy started with about twenty or so volunteers, then he cut it down to ten, eliminating the mother, then cut it down to six. Then he did all the usual things they do with the deeply hypnotized. Making them do foolish stuff. Making them dance like ballerinas, play invisible musical instruments, walk like chickens, and act like various other animals, and so on. Then the guy tripped on the stage, smashed his head, and was knocked unconscious."

"With the six still 'under'?"

"Exactly. When they finally revived the guy, after about forty-five minutes, he did his best to pull the six volunteers out of their trances. But Bryan was convinced that Tory was still 'under' when he met her."

"Is that possible?"

"It is. The first rule of hypnosis is to make sure that the subject is completely 'out' of the trance. There've been numerous cases of people acting oddly afterward because they're still 'under suggestion.' For example, they might be in the supermarket and get triggered by something and start dancing around the aisles like a ballerina."

"Is it dangerous?"

"Rarely. I looked it up once. There are a few creepy anecdotal cases out there. A couple that supposedly led to mental imbalance."

"Did the girl do anything odd?"

"Not as far as I know."

"What happened?"

"Bryan was concerned, so he read a few books about hypnotism, and he 'snapped' her out of it."

"Are you buying any of this?"

He gave his little shrug again.

"Not really."

"Tell me something else. Something odd."

"Bryan once told me that they never had sex. That they were waiting. But he also told me that they were both having the same exact dream where they would rendezvous beneath the boardwalk at the Jersey Shore and make love. He told me that they were both having the same dream. Separately. Eventually, when they talked about it, they learned that their dreams were *exactly* the same. Same clothes, same boardwalk, same weather, same everything."

"They sound like a pair of weirdos."

Maybe I should have been more tactful, but he didn't take offense.

"I think they were, in a way, and her death really messed him up, but it also gave purpose to his life."

"What purpose?"

"A spiritual quest. Before Tory died, she said something to Bryan on her deathbed, which I believe directed his entire subsequent life."

"What did she say?"

"He never told me, but he'd been on some kind of spiritual journey ever since."

It was time to get back to the murder in Barnegat Light.

"You never actually met Chloe Hathaway?"

"No."

"What about Zoe Hathaway?"

"Never. I sent flowers to the wake. And a sympathy email to both Zoe and Bryan."

"Do you have any idea why he killed himself?"

"No. I suppose he couldn't handle losing Chloe. Losing someone he loved. Which had happened before. But I don't believe, Mr. Colt, for a single second, that he'd ever hurt that girl. The girl he told me he'd 'fallen madly in love with.'"

"It happens."

"Bryan wouldn't hurt anyone."

"Well, he definitely hurt himself."

Singh said nothing.

"How much are you getting?" I asked.

Xander had hacked the will.

It was another rude question, but sometimes they're very effective.

"A lot, apparently. Everything he had. But I had absolutely no idea that I was in Bryan's will. I certainly don't need the money."

I stood up and looked down at the little man behind his big desk.

"I'm sorry I'm so unpleasant, but I have a murder to solve."

"I understand, Mr. Colt. I'd like to see things resolved as well."

I believed him, nodded, and left his office. Down in the lobby, I texted Nonna:

> See if Andrew Blake is still alive.
> See if Singh was in surgery early yesterday morning.
> Thanks.

26. LAX

THE NEXT flight to LAX was 7:10 p.m.

When I boarded the Boeing 757, holding my copy of *Wuthering Heights*, the seat next to mine was already occupied.

"What the hell are you doing here?"

"I'm sticking with you, pal."

It was a pretty young woman with big glasses.

"Like I don't have enough problems."

She stepped into the aisle so I took my seat next to the window. When we were settled, I looked at my travel companion, into her glasses, into her ambers.

"This has nothing to do with Sykes," I said.

She shrugged as if it didn't make any difference.

"Who cares? I'm coming to California."

I laughed. In spite of myself.

"I thought I was flying alone. With Emily Brontë."

"Instead, you're flying with both of us."

"How'd you find me?"

"Nonna said you were flying to LA."

"And the flight info?"

"I work for the FBI."

Later, when we were twenty thousand feet in the air, I asked her about her wound.

"It hurts. I've never been shot before."

I gave her a compliment.

"I like your new getup. I thought you slept every night in your fed suit."

She was wearing tight jeans, navy sneakers, a pink button-down cotton blouse, and a red NYU windbreaker.

With big glasses.

She looked, pardon the expression, adorable.

"Look who's talking! You *always* wear the same suit. Which I hope is not the *exact same* Armani suit. I hope you've got a closet full of them."

"I do."

We talked about the case, and I told her where I was at.

"So why are we going to California?"

"I have no idea why *you're* going to California."

But at least I knew she'd be safe for a while.

"So why are *you* going to California?" she tried again.

I decided to tell her.

Actually, I didn't have much choice.

"A friend of mine is in the hospital. A close friend. I got the call around five o'clock and drove straight to the airport."

"A girl?"

"Yes."

"Tell me what you want to tell me, Colt."

So I did.

It wasn't easy.

Because the backstory's so complicated.

I told her that I'd met Roxs Faulkner three years ago when I was working a case in LA, a case that ended up in Marina del Rey. Leaving out all of the interesting parts, I explained that Roxs later came to New Jersey to work as my secretary/researcher. But there was a "problem" (undelineated), so she went back home to Hermosa Beach three months ago. Then we communicated for a while; then it faded out.

"Why's she in the hospital?"

"A surfing accident. Her board smacked her in the head."

"Is it bad?"

"Probably. She has a history of head trauma. She was once in a terrible car crash on the Pacific Coast Highway."

"Are you in love with her?"

"I was."

She went silent.

The interrogation was over.

She wanted to think about things. Lots of things. Maybe even the story I'd just told her, which was the Cliffs Notes version of the real story.

"I'm exhausted," she admitted.

"You look it."

She shut her eyes.

I opened Emily Brontë.

III

Somebody wrote a book called Weird NJ. *It was the only state that required a second volume.*

— Thomas C. Colt

27. Hermosa Beach

Monday, May 16th
66°

Y<small>OU'RE IN</small> love with that girl."

Sleeping Beauty had risen from her princess bed.

I was standing on the balcony of our suite in the Beach House Hotel, staring past the Strand at a distant young woman in a lovely pink bathing suit, sitting on a blue blanket beneath a brightly colored, multi-striped beach umbrella, reading a book.

Wearing shades against the early morning Pacific sun.

Naturally, she was facing the ocean, so I couldn't see the bandage on her forehead.

Yes, she was far off in the distance, but I knew every detail. Tall, thin, athletic, twenty-five, with short-cropped black hair and green, green eyes. Looking more than a little bit like a young Audrey Hepburn.

Who'd been a collegiate volleyball star.

Who'd been a researcher for LAPD.

Who'd worked for me.

Standing right behind me was my traveling companion.

Last night, when we arrived at LAX, I called Henry Faulkner, Roxs's father.

"You shouldn't have come."

"I heard she's at UCLA Med."

"She's out."

"Can I see her?"

"Why don't we talk tomorrow morning?"

"Where?"

"The beach."

Then I called the Beach House Hotel to change my reservation to a suite with two bedrooms.

No problem.

Then we cabbed to the hotel.

Me and Miss Sleepyhead.

I wondered if she'd slept at all since her sister was murdered six days ago. When we got to Hermosa, she was out like a light, so I carried her to her bedroom. She was light as a feather. Like a fairy princess.

With a Glock 17M.

I put her on the bed, gently, took off her windbreaker, took off her sneakers, and shut the door.

It was now almost eight o'clock in the morning, and she was standing behind me, watching me watch the girl on the beach.

"Maybe," I said, for further clarification.

While Zoe was sleeping last night, I was out on the moors running around with Catherine and Heathcliff. It's a weird-ass book, and I've always preferred her sister's *Jane Eyre*. By a long shot. What guy wouldn't want a Jane Eyre in his life?

But *Heights* is something else. Oddly structured, oddly plotted, and filled with unlikable characters. Many detestable. None of which helped the Olivier-Oberon film version of 1939.

But my primary interest was its "soulmate" thing.

Yeah, it's true that Catherine says:

"I am Heathcliff!"

Also:

"He's more myself than I am."

Also:

"Whatever our souls are made of, his and mine are the same."

I hate to say it, but I think Catherine's a load of crap. Yeah, she's passionate about her childhood bonding with Heathcliff, but she's even more attracted by the upper-class Lintons and all their genteel superficialities. When all's said and done, she throws over her boorish, vulgar, vengeful, hateful, diabolical Heathcliff for shallow Edgar Linton.

So much for "soulmateishness."

"Shared souls."

Give me Miss Jane Eyre.

Maybe dopey Heathcliff really believed that Catherine Earnshaw was his "soulmate," but it takes two to tango. Besides, the guy's clearly deranged. Personally, I don't understand why anybody would want to be soulmates with either one of them.

So the book wasn't much help.

I suspect that Bryan Sykes and Tory Blake were much closer to the real thing, but Tory died at fifteen, and who knows what would have happened if she hadn't.

By the way, this isn't some kind of hey-I'm-a-tough-guy-so-I'm-anti-romantic. Despite my appearance, I'm as mushy as the next guy when it comes to the contrasting/complementary sex. Hell, I'd stood on the balcony for nearly half an hour, hoping that Roxanne would show up and spread her blue blanket over her favorite spot at Hermosa Beach.

When room service arrived, we had a nice breakfast together. Zoe looked lovely. Refreshed. *Very* lovely, in fact. Then I realized she was sans glasses.

"Where's the spectacles?"

"In my room. I get the impression you prefer me without them."

"I prefer you either way."

She smiled, then remembered the girl on the beach.

"I thought she was in the hospital?"

"They let her out."

"Have you talked to her yet?"

"No. I'm meeting her old man at nine o'clock."

Half an hour later, we left the hotel and walked to a bench on the Strand, facing the ocean.

"Hermosa," as you probably know, means "beautiful."

Hermosa Beach is exactly that.

So beautiful, in fact, that it could be a beach down the Jersey Shore. As could Manhattan Beach to the north. As could Redondo Beach to the south. Up near the pier, kids were playing volleyball in the sand. Down to the south, a handful of surfers were waiting for bigger waves. There was still a morning mist in the air, known locally as "May gray," but the sunbathers were starting to show up and spread their blankets. These uncrowded early mornings were always Roxs's favorite. Peaceful. With a muted sun, with the never-ending sound of the ocean waves.

Henry Faulkner was sitting on a white bench as we approached.

Back in the California "Part I" of my relationship with his daughter, Henry was, oddly enough, never a problem. Despite my profession, despite my appearance, he actually seemed to like me. So did his wife. They'd obviously decided that I was "good for Roxs," which always amazed me, but I was grateful.

Henry, as usual, was California casual. Light cotton slacks, a light-blue polo, and deck shoes. He was some kind of administrator at USC. He didn't actually run the place, but he had a big-time job of some kind, and the family lived very comfortably near the beach.

Until I came along.

He stood up.

Always a likable, friendly man.

"It's good to see you, Chris."

We shook hands.

"This is Special Agent Zoe Hathaway."

Henry and Zoe shook hands, then Zoe walked away, up the Strand toward the pier.

"What's going on, Henry?"

He sat down.

"It's happened again, Chris."

Maybe I should take a moment to explain this "Chris" business, just as I would later need to explain it to Zoe. Back when I first met Roxs at the Hard Rock Cafe in Los Angeles, I was using my west coast alias. "Christopher Colt." It was something that my uncle had set up many years ago, and it proved to be extremely useful in a number of cases, especially the runaways that led me to the West Coast.

As a result, Roxs and her parents knew me as "Chris."

I sat down.

"Tell me."

"It's the same damned thing all over again, Chris. Just like the car crash. She banged her head on the surfboard, and she's forgotten again."

It's called Selective Retrograde Amnesia, something about messing up the hippocampus and the neural pathways. It happened when that stupid kid crashed her on the Pacific Coast Highway two years ago.

Severe head trauma.

The first time it happened, it wiped out *all* her memories of the past year or so. In other words, it wiped out *me*. Our entire California relationship. "Part I."

"How far back?"

"About a year and a half. It's a bit worse than the last time."

Meaning me again. The entire New Jersey "Part II" phase of our relationship.

When she worked in my office in Paterson.

"It sounds ridiculous."

"Well, her doctors say it's not that unlikely. Especially since she's now got a 'propensity.'"

"Does she know who I am?"

"No."

I stared across the sand.

The pretty amnesiac put down her book and was heading to the ocean. She always liked a quick, brisk, early morning jump in the Pacific.

"Should she be getting her head wet?"

"No. She won't."

She didn't.

But the waves splashed almost to her shoulders.

"I hate to say this, Chris, and please forgive me, but I think you need to leave her alone. Put her behind you. That life that you might have hoped for, that Roxanne might have hoped for, is never going to happen."

He was right, and I knew it, but it hurt.

A lot.

I'm immune to a lot of stuff, but not that kind of hurt.

"I believe," he continued, gently, "from what I understand, that you two put an end to things a few months ago."

"It was still somewhat up in the air."

"I'm sorry, Chris."

"Will you call me if she remembers?"

"Yes."

I waited for more, for some kind of assurance.

"If things change, I'll call you, Chris. I promise. But even if she starts to remember again, I'm not sure it'll lead to anything."

He was probably right.

"All right," I said.

He stood up.

"It was good of you to come, Chris, but it's something that we'll have to deal with on our own. We'll take good care of her."

I had no doubt.

"Burn the surfboard."

"It's already gone."

He walked away, south on the Strand, with nothing but thoughts about how to protect his beloved daughter.

Who emerged from the ocean in the same pink bathing suit that she bought at the New Jersey Shore.

To please me.

But those days were over.

If I walked up to her right now, she'd have no idea who I was. She might even be frightened.

I watched her dry her lovely self off before sitting down with her book again.

I wondered what it was.

I wondered a lot of things.

Eventually, my federal agent came back.

"What's up, Jack?"

I stood up.

"It's time to go."

"You sure?"

She looked across the sand at the pink girl reading her book. Zoe was doing her very best to be kind, to give me whatever time I needed.

"Yeah, let's go."

"Where?"

28. Scottsdale

WHO *ARE* YOU?"

I think he already knew.

"Have a seat," I said.

He'd just come in the front door of his modest log cabin and found me sitting in one of the comfortable chairs facing his comfortable couch. I liked the place. Lots of wood, with nice dark furniture, with nice mahogany gun racks.

I unholstered my Python and placed it down on the coffee table between us.

He took a seat on the couch.

"You packing?" I asked.

"No."

I believed him.

He wore black jeans, a black polo, a black windbreaker, and a black baseball cap.

With an SF Giants logo.

"I wish it was preseason," I said, "I'd like to take in a game. I'm a big fan."

Football's always been number one with me, but baseball's close behind. Maybe one-and-a-half. Tied with the sweet science.

After Hermosa, we flew from LAX to Phoenix.

"Why Arizona?" she asked.

"A quick pit stop."

"Fine."

"Then it's back to Jersey."

Meaning back to the two cases.

"Sounds good."

On the short flight, Nonna sent me her "suspect" list. Actually two of them. She's a big Hercule Poirot fan, and she likes to list the suspects "According to Grandma Salerno."

"With commentary."

I've never minded.

I actually look forward to it.

The Garvey Murder:

Savannah Garvey (unless you've been smitten)
Daniel Garvey (the loser son)
Kimberly Watts (yeah, I know, a bit of a stretch)
Matthew Harker (I'm betting on this one)
Travis Turner (too stupid)
Angela Rossini (too something)
Francesco Ravello (why not? put him on all the lists)
Carlos Cortez (but something's "off")
Joey Greco (do goons like him commit murder?)
Lukacs Papp (no way)

I enjoyed it.

Even the word "smitten."

The Hathaway Murder:

Bryan Sykes (everybody's favorite)
Zoe Hathaway (it happens, John)

Raven Davenport (who knows what was going on at work?)
Mrs. Newman (leave this one alone)
Camille Anderson (never trust wealthy bitches)
Dr. Singh (the winner on my list)
Andrew Blake (if not dead already)
Anybody else I don't know about?

Maybe I should give her my PI badge?

I rented a Lincoln MKZ in Phoenix, and we drove through the Valley of the Sun into beautiful Scottsdale, "the west's most western town," whatever that means, and a major player in the Cactus League.

I headed right for Scottsdale Stadium.

The last preseason game, Giants 6, Diamondbacks 4, was long past March 23. But I wanted to see the place. Red brick. Wrought iron. Classic. Intimate. In historic Old Town, in the Sonoran Desert, in front of Camelback Mountain. I bribed a guard with a fifty, and my befuddled companion and I walked out onto the field.

Is there anything more beautiful than a baseball field?

The green grass, the diamond, the blue sky.

"You ever play?" I wondered.

"I was a pretty lousy athlete."

I tried to be polite about it.

"There's more to life than sports."

But I couldn't resist adding:

"But not much."

She smiled.

A pretty smile.

I think she was enjoying our inexplicable "pit stop." I think she was glad to get away from the East Coast for a while and put her sister's murder on hold. Probably because she was confident I'd figure it out.

"You'll get him, Colt. I know you will."

To be honest, I've never lacked confidence, but it felt good anyway.

We drove to Marker's house, and I left her inside the rental. I never spotted the guy at the ballpark, where he worked, which was good. I wanted to talk to him in private.

"It's a thousand degrees out here!" she complained.

A bit of an exaggeration, especially sitting in an air-conditioned Lincoln.

Ten minutes later, I came back to the car carrying something in a green trash bag.

I put it in the back seat.

"Something looks like a rifle."

"Don't touch it, Miss Fed. I'll explain when I come back."

She didn't say a word, which surprised me, so I went back into the house and waited.

Marker nodded.

"It's a great job. Actually, it's a great life."

He didn't seem frightened at all, more the stoic type.

Like me.

I liked him.

"A woman?"

"Not at the moment. That's the flaw in my life."

I understood.

The front door opened and guess-who walked inside.

"I'm not missing any of this," she said. "Whatever the hell it is."

I smiled.

Even Marker smiled.

I pointed at the chair to my right. Glasses sat down.

She was packing her Glock.

Good girl.

"Not a word," I said.

She put her finger to her lips.

Mostly to bust my chops, which I enjoyed, then I looked back at Marker.

"Pamela Hopkins asked me to look into the death of her daughter."

"Sure, the mother bitch."

It was more than bitter.

"I've got your Mauser M18 in the back of my rental. It's nicely constructed for the price."

He agreed, nodding.

"Yeah, a bargain."

"I've also got your flight records to Newark, then back again, last week."

I wanted him to know he was trapped like a rat.

He knew.

"Who are you?"

"I guess my 'fame' didn't quite extend to Maricopa County in the middle of the desert.

"I'm a private dick. I was standing in front of your brother when he blew his brains out."

Now he knew who I was.

His older brother, Bryan Marker, born in New Jersey, had been the head of Governor Hopkins' security detail. Then he fell under the spell of the governor's daughter and started killing people.

Including himself, rather than ratting her out.

From what Nonna had scrounged up, Eric Marker idolized his older brother and followed him into the Marines where he discovered he was quite a marksman. When he left the corps, he did what his brother did. He went into private security. Eventually, he ended up with the gig at the stadium.

"You were clean up to the Brownstone," I pointed out.

He shrugged.

"He was my brother."

Personally, I never liked his brother. He was a bit too slick, a bit too cocky. He was one of those guys who gave you the feeling that he was "up" to something. Something not good.

Which he was.

Thumping the governor's daughter then doing her dirty work.

Including murder.

"I'm taping this," I said.

"Of course you are," he said.

The guy was no idiot.

He looked over at my traveling companion.

"What's she?"

It sounded more confused than condescending.

"She's invisible," I said.

"She looks like a librarian."

Then he caught himself and clarified.

"A very pretty one."

"Thanks," said the invisible librarian.

It was time to wrap things up.

"Let me ask you the stupidest question I could possibly ask. *Why* did you kill Meredith Hopkins in the alley near the Brownstone?"

"You know why."

"I'd like to have it on tape."

He complied.

"I shot Meredith Hopkins because she destroyed my brother's life. Also, let me say for the record, even though I'm not exactly sure what kind of 'record' this is, that I'm sorry for having shot her security guys."

"The shots were nicely placed," I assured him. "They're both doing fine."

He appreciated the update.

"The target moved at the last minute, when I had the crosshairs on her forehead. So I had to take the other guys out. Then I had to wait for her to stick her stupid head above the limo again. It didn't take long. Then I popped her. It felt good."

He looked at me.

Intensely.

"She deserved it."

I couldn't disagree.

"How long do I have?" he asked.

"I don't know."

Which I said because I really didn't know the answer.

29. Stone Tower

Tuesday, May 17th
54°

I T'S NOT over.
Of course it's not.
The old man squirmed in his bed, in pain, sitting up partially.
What do you need?
Some water.
I got him a glass from the sink, and he sipped it slowly.
Bread and water?
I was kidding.
Pizza and Coke.
He looked at me. With the same scrutinizing Jesuit look that he often used with his last remaining relative.
It's an interesting story, Johnny boy, but you're obviously using it to duck the real story.
I played dumb.
What are you talking about?
You know what I'm talking about. What happened in California?
How do you know about that?
He shrugged.

Of course! Nonna had obviously ratted me out.

What happened?

So I told him.

Most of it.

He listened with uncharacteristic silence, then drew his conclusions.

I have to agree with Mr. Faulkner. The poor girl's brain is damaged, and you might make things worse. She needs bedrest. She needs brainrest.

And beachrest.

Have you accepted it?

Yes.

Then he looked at me askance.

A good word for a ninety-eight-year-old.

What's the deal with that pretty fed you're running around with?

Note to self: strangle Nonna.

Answer the question.

Nothing. No "deal" at all.

I hear she's rather pretty, in a curious kind of way.

Can a man fire his best friend's grandmother?

He paid no attention.

Are you sure?

I think I shrugged.

I'm never sure about anything relating to women.

I'm afraid she's developing a taste for you, John. Almost as bad, I think she's developing a taste for danger. The young woman should go back to her cubicle. She's not a "street" agent.

I didn't know what to say.

He pressed forward.

And what's the deal with pretty Savannah Garvey?

No deal.

You sure?

No deal.

I didn't know if I was lying or not.

Didn't your Uncle Tom teach you that lying's a sin?

Let's get back to Bryan Sykes and Tory Blake.

Fine.

30. Culver's Lake

THAT'S A weird-ass house."

Which I said to myself, out loud.

It was actually two small wooden houses, identical, both painted hunter green, conjoined over a narrow driveway by a wooden walkway from the upstairs of the one house to the upstairs of the other.

"What is it?" Zoe asked.

"It's the 'house in the woods.' Where Sykes and Tory grew up together. With him on the left, with his father, with Tory on the right, with her mother."

"When they were in love?"

"Yes."

Sykes had, apparently, never sold the twin houses, maybe out of loyalty to his youth, to his tragic past. To Tory. He always used Surf City as his permanent address, although he had condos in Princeton, Bernardsville, and Manhattan. Money was obviously no problem. But for some reason, he'd asked Wendy Newman to mail the silver ring up here, to rural Sussex, to Culver's Lake, which is less than a mile away, 555 acres of spring-fed waters, deep in the Kittatinny Mountains.

I parked in the driveway.

"Containing all the secrets?"

"I hope so, Zoe. Let's find out."

We went to the front door of the Sykes house on the left.

"Look the other way."

She did. She understood.

I jimmied the door, and we went inside. It was darkish but not uncomfortable. It looked like a house that had been dormant for a hundred years, which wasn't the case. We roamed through the place until we found the study, lined with file cabinets.

I think Zoe was enjoying herself.

"Where do we start?"

I pulled out the top drawer on the far-left cabinet.

Like the drawers beneath it, it was filled with thick files, each marked with a woman's name. The files included multifarious documentations of their individual lives: birth records, surreptitious photographs from all ages, medical reports, school records, transcripts, etc.

"The files at Hoover aren't this thorough."

She was amazed.

So was I.

The last file cabinet was entirely dedicated to Tory Blake, fully documenting everything documentable in her fifteen short years. Including her death certificate with the name of the doctor who called her TOD. Her time of death.

It was like a paper memorial.

A strange tribute.

Zoe was staring at countless Tory photographs, particularly a headshot.

In color.

"She looks like me!"

"Like us," she added, including her dead sister.

She meant the eyes.

Amber gold.

"Is that it?" she wondered. "Did the guy have an insane obsession with amber eyes?"

"I think there's a lot more to it than that."

As for me, I was thumbing through the files for Camille, for Wendy, and for Chloe. Overall, there were about twenty-five females who were meticulously documented.

Surreptitiously.

Twenty-five young women, all the same age, all from the New York metro area, who had no idea that a madman had spent the past twenty-five years of his life meticulously tracking all their significant milestones. Spending endless time, spending endless money.

For what?

"I'm going next door."

Zoe nodded, completely engulfed in the tsunami of Sykes's obsessions.

Outside, I got a text from Xander.

1.) I put the GPS on the Lexus last night
2.) Cortez's mom put a deposit on a condo in Hillcrest
3.) Greco's wife volunteers at the Innocence Project

Just like Xander.

Efficient as always.

Even "numbered."

Quickly, I checked the GPS app that Xander had sent me.

Fine, the Lexus was exactly where it was supposed to be.

Then I jimmied the door at the Blake house and went inside. It was similar to the other house, obviously built by the same builder, but there were obvious female touches. Doily place mats, unlit scented candles, empty vases, and pretty landscapes on the walls, mostly mysterious-

looking sunsets. A bit New Ageish. Over near the fireplace there
was a comfortable armchair covered with a cable-knit throw. I had
no doubt that it was the chair where the dead Debbie Sykes was
sitting when Bryan came to see her the morning after the burial of
the love of his life.

I also had no doubt that nobody had ever sat in the chair since
that day.

The entire house was like a memorial museum, without a tour
guide. A period piece. Probably untouched in twenty-five years. In
tribute to the young Tory Blake.

I went upstairs to her bedroom. It was perfectly neat. Spotless.
With a young girl's white vanity, a little wooden desk, and a closet
full of ordinary teenage clothes.

And a bed.

Oddly unmade.

It looked like someone had lain in the bed not that long ago.
It reminded me of the scene in *Psycho* when Vera Miles goes into
the mother's bedroom.

Is it too weird to imagine that Sykes occasionally slept in Tory's
bed, attempting to be "close" to his dead soulmate?

On the night table, there were two framed pictures. One of
Tory and her mother, one of Sykes and Tory. All smiling.

It was sad.

Creepy.

If the rest of the house was a museum, this room was a shrine.

I looked closer at the night table. There were several rings, five
small silver rings, and an old book by some guy named Ashland
Cox, whom I'd never heard of.

I opened the book to the title page. Someone had written:

For you.

For me?

I doubted it.

Nonna called.

"Andrew Blake is alive."

I was standing in his dead daughter's bedroom.

"Where?"

"Ossining. For murder."

I looked at my watch. Culver's Lake was about an hour-and-a-half drive to the prison.

Nonna was still on the line waiting for her thanks.

"Great job, Nonna. There's something else."

"Of course, there is."

She waited.

"I'd like you to track down Dr. Zachary Sullivan, the doctor who called the TOD at Tory's deathbed at Newton Medical Center. And any nurses in the room at the time."

"What would you do without me?"

"Live a more peaceful life."

She laughed.

I kept the book, left Tory's room, and went down the staircase. Then back to Sykes's house. Zoe was completely surrounded with files, with paper, with photographs. It looked like a whirlwind had whipped through the room.

"Is this what your DC office looks like?"

She paid no attention.

She looked up, stunned by everything around her.

In disbelief.

"He was tracking these girls for twenty-five years."

"Yes."

"Is this what it seems to be?"

"Yes."

31. Sing Sing

Tuesday, May 17th
57°

WHY'D HE COME?"

I was sitting in a small conference room with David Crockett.

Yeah, Davy Crockett.

Aka Andrew Blake.

Sometimes in this racket, things actually work out.

Usually not, but occasionally.

I called the Governor's office from Culver's Lake, and they called the warden across the river who set up the sit-down. Sometimes it helps to have connections in high places.

Sometimes it also helps to have an illegal hacker on staff. Xander was able to access the prison's visitor logs for David Crockett, which were mostly blank except for a visit from Bryan Sykes about fifteen years ago.

Naturally, I wanted to know what *that* was all about.

Andrew Blake was a sixty-two-year-old tough guy, looking twenty years older, squat, baldish, wearing his gray prison uniform, with booze-wearied features and dumb tattoos. One located on his forehead. Four letters. "TORY." The guy was pathetic. He'd abandoned his pretty wife and his one-year-old daughter about forty years ago, changed his name to David Crockett and moved to Poughkeepsie, New York, for construction work. Apparently, it didn't pay enough. Several years later, he got involved in several big-time warehouse robberies, killing a security guard in the last one. It was cold-blooded, maybe meth-accelerated, and it got him "life without" at Sing Sing's max prison.

The old prison, which opened back in 1826, packed in about two thousand super-losers these days. All sent "up the river" to Ossining, New York, thirty miles north of New York City, overlooking the Hudson River. Which is where the expression comes from. "Up the river." Somewhere, hidden down in the basement (now retired), is "Old Sparky," which fried 614 men and women over the years. Making "life without" sound like a walk in the park.

Which, as I was waiting for "Mr. Crockett," got me thinking about death again, about Uncle Tom's "last words" list, about some of the more disheartening ones:

"All is dark and doubtful."—Edward Gibbon, historian

"All my possessions for one moment of time."—Elizabeth I, Queen of England

"Let my epitaph be: 'Here lies Joseph, who was unsuccessful in all his undertakings.'"—Joseph II, Habsburg-Lorraine, Holy Roman Emperor

"I had provided for everything in my life except death, and now, alas! I am to die, though entirely unprepared."—Cesare Borgia

And maybe the most pathetic of all:

"What have I lived for?"—Lorenz Hart, lyricist

As for me, I hope to go out like GW:

"I am not afraid to die."—George Washington

Before leaving Culver's Lake, I made Zoe promise to drive straight to the FBI field office in Federal Plaza and wait for me there.

"Why?"

"So I can tell your bosses everything I know."

"Do you know *everything*, Colt?"

"Almost."

Then I drove to Ossining, strolled into Sing Sing, and finally, was sitting across a gray metal table from Andrew Blake.

Who answered my question.

"He wanted to talk about Tory."

"I thought you were out of the picture for the past forty years?"

"I was."

"What did he ask about?"

"Her birth."

"Meaning what?"

"He wanted to know if anything unusual happened."

"Did it?"

He shrugged.

"She had a PDA."

Which is a condition that I knew something about because Luca's first kid was born with a PDA. It's some kind of messed up opening between the aorta and the pulmonary artery leading away from the heart. It can get the blood flowing in the wrong direction, and it can also do damage to the heart. Usually, as with Luca's kid, it closes off naturally after a few days, but if it doesn't, it can be a serious problem. Leading to pulmonary hypertension, lung damage, heart infection, or heart failure. Sometimes requiring surgical closure.

A few hours ago, when I was scanning the various medical reports in Sykes's files, I noticed that some of the girls had PDAs.

Maybe all of them did.

"What happened?"

"It closed in a couple of weeks. Long before I left."

"What else?"

"I finally told the guy to beat it. I don't get many visitors. Actually, I get none. But the guy was creeping me out. Why was he so interested in Tory's birth? So I sent him packing. I even told him to 'get a life.' Which I realize sounds pretty ironic coming from me."

"Why'd you change your name?"

"I wanted a new start in life."

"As Davy Crockett?"

"Yeah, why not?"

"Yeah, why not?" I agreed.

"Obviously, it didn't work out too well."

"Do you have regrets?"

I sounded like a priest, but I was curious.

"I'm nothing but regret."

Adding.

"And remorse."

"Did you ever see Tory again after you left Culver's Lake?"

"Never, but I've thought about her every single day. And I never thought I had the right to walk back into her life. Besides, I had nothing to offer."

"Love?" I tried, sounding like a hack therapist.

He shrugged, and I left it alone.

"Did you ever," I continued, "see Debbie Blake again after you left Culver's Lake?"

"Never. She drove me crazy with all that New Age crap. Psychics, meditations, candles, charts, and all the rest of it. But she was still a good woman, who deserved a lot better than me."

He was right about that.

"Did she ever find it?" he wondered out loud.

"I don't know. She never married again."

"I screwed up everything."

He was right about that as well, and I tried not to feel sorry for the moron. After all, he was a cold-blooded killer.

But I thanked him anyway.

Then I left his prison, "Losersville," got in my XTS, and checked the GPS app.

Good, the Lexus was sitting right where it was supposed to be.

I called Zoe.

"Are you at the field office?"

"Yes."

"I should be down there in about an hour and a half."

She was pleased.

"I'm on the fourth floor. Room 422."

I shut off my cell, turned on the Boss, then hit the Taconic State Parkway, cruising comfortably.

When I hit downtown, it was the usual mess, but the Boss was singing, "Back in Your Arms" from the *Tracks* album," one of my favorites:

> And all the love I've thrown away and lost
> I'm longin' for again
> Now darlin' I just want to be back in your arms
> Back in your arms again.

When it ended, I shut him off and checked the GPS again.

Damn it!

The Lexus was sitting in Federal Plaza!
I was five blocks away.
At Canal and Broad.

32. Federal Plaza

Tuesday, May 17th
58°

I DROVE LIKE a lunatic.

Screeching to the curb, onto the curb, behind a red Lexus.

Next to the Delta bollards, the high-security barriers in front of 26 Federal Plaza.

Pedestrians scattered, a few with choice remarks.

I rushed to the entrance, then through the metal detector. When the alarm went off, I tased the guard to the ground. I could see her in the elevator.

But the doors closed.

Before the guard revived and tried to shoot me in the back, I found the stairs and raced, two at a time, to the fourth floor. The stairwell door was locked, so I pulled out my Python and blew it open.

Not a good idea in a building full of two thousand FBI agents. I rushed down the corridor, holding up my meaningless badge, yelling, over and over:

"Federal Marshall! Federal Marshall!"

What's worse?

Parking illegally in Manhattan?

Assaulting an armed guard?

Impersonating a Federal Marshall?

Everything was happening so fast that no one tried to tackle me. Or shoot me.

Everyone was confused.

When I found room 422, I heard a buzzing sound.

The door was locked.

I blew it apart.

Zoe was lying on the floor of a small office, with small windows overlooking lower Manhattan.

She was lying on the rug.

Tased, stunned.

Camille was kneeling over her. Her knife was out. She'd already grabbed Zoe by the hair, ready to stab her under the chin, as she'd done with Chloe.

It seemed easier to kick her than shoot her.

I kicked her under her left arm, into her chest.

It was a heavy kick. *Very* heavy. No one would want to be kicked with a kick like that.

Camille flew across the small room into the far wall, ending up on her back, looking up at me.

With hate.

I'm sure you've all seen "hate" of one kind or another in your lives. But this was "psychopath" hate, which is something above and beyond.

"You ugly creep!"

I've been called a "creep" before, many times in fact, and tons of other negative stuff, but I've never been called "ugly."

What's the expression? There's no accounting for taste.

She reached for her purse and pulled out her Sig Sauer. Which looked like a P320. Which, surely, was the gun that killed Wendy Newman.

I wondered if she was planning to shoot me first or shoot Zoe first. It must have been a tough choice.

I blew a hole through her left shoulder.

She looked down at the expanding red spot on her white summer jacket. Which began dripping. She seemed fascinated by the concept.

The P320 had dropped, and Zoe grabbed it.

Then Zoe stood up.

"Look at her eyes," she said.

Yes, they were "psycho" eyes, but they were also golden.

Amber.

Very beautiful.

Later, quite a bit later, I was looking at another pair of ambers on a bench in Central Park near Gapstow Bridge. Evening was falling over the greatest park in the world, and everything was lovely.

She took off her glasses.

She kissed me.

Nicely.

"Was that a 'thank you' kiss? Or something more?"

"I don't know. What do you want it to be?"

"I don't know."

I had absolutely no idea.

The old priest was right about me vis-à-vis the lovely sex.

"I don't want to go back to DC," she decided.

"You like getting tased?" I kidded.

She smiled.

"Maybe I do."

She reflected a moment, then continued.

"I used to love my job, Colt."

Then she looked at me directly, eyes to eyes, eyes to shades.

"Hire me?"

I'm *never* at a loss for words, but I was at a loss for words.

"You're my Shane, Jack Colt," she kidded.

"He rode away in the end," I reminded her.

"Yeah, to Paterson, New Jersey."

I laughed.

"Hire me, Colt."

33. Stone Tower

Tuesday, May 17th
54°

L ET'S GET back to Bryan Sykes and Tory Blake.
   Fine.

Fine.

So the kid's now rolling in bucks.

Yeah, but on the surface, at least, he does what most kids do. He finishes high school; then he heads off to college. Rutgers. Where his parents met. Double-majoring in psychology and world religions.

I guess he's got issues.

I guess it would be impossible not to. He'd seen his mother, his father, his girlfriend, and Tory's mother all die in front of him before he was sixteen. So it would make some sense that he was searching for answers.

Any religion in his past?

Nothing much. It seems that his dad, after his wife's death, was a pretty mushy non-churchgoing "Christian," and, of course, Tory's mom was into all kinds of New Age mumbo jumbo.

Hmm.

But Bryan did well at RU, rooming with a premed kid, Krish Singh. Then he got a fellowship, which he really didn't need, to the University of Virginia, where he studied with Ian Stevenson, the Carlson Professor of Psychiatry at the School of Medicine. Who was one of the world's most famous researchers of the paranormal.

I'm assuming that all of this will somehow "tie together" in the end. Right?

Right. But we have to go back to the death of Tory Blake.

To the hospital?

Yes. Nonna tracked down Dr. Zachary Sullivan, the doctor who called Tory's Time of Death, but the man had died years ago. Then Nonna also tracked down one of the nurses, Missy Edwards, who's now retired and living in Milton.

Because you're after the "last words," right?

Right, and when I talked to Missy Edwards on the phone, she remembered it "like it was yesterday." It's not often that a nurse gets to see a young girl die of Legionnaires' disease. She told me that Tory looked at Bryan, who was holding her hand, and said, "Find me. I won't be far." Which, it seems, motivated the entire rest of Sykes's life. Obsessively.

Is this going where I think it's going?

Yes, Bryan Sykes spent the rest of his life tracking down girls he thought might be his reincarnated lover.

Whoa!

Yeah, whoa!

But why'd he wait twenty-five years?

Hey, not so fast, holy man. Let's go back to the burial.

To the other missing conversation?

Yeah, because standing over the grave of her young daughter, Debbie Blake looked at young Sykes and said, "Find her."

Just like her daughter.

Just like her daughter. Then she told Sykes to begin searching, but to wait "twenty-five years." Then they were interrupted.

So the next day he went to her house to ask her why, and she was already dead in her chair.

Exactly, but there was a book in her lap. Well-worn and heavily annotated. Bryan picked it up. Then he turned to the title page, where she'd written, "For you." The book was *Metempsychosis*: a short, concise book about reincarnation by Ashland Cox, a professor of Asiatic Studies at the University of London. The book was published by a small British press in 1975, and Cox died in a Bath retirement home in 1985. The Cox book became Sykes's "bible."

How do you know all this stuff?

Camille told me earlier today at the FBI field office. Somehow she figured out what Sykes was up to, and he decided to confide in her.

A big mistake.

A big mistake.

Tell me more about the book.

Cox promoted the concept of "instantaneous" reincarnation, meaning the person's soul, "*atman*," transfers at the *exact* time of death into a concurrent newborn. Thus the time of death is crucial. Some Eastern religions believe in the "conception" theory, meaning transferal at conception. Others believe in a "delayed state" theory, meaning that the transfer can take place at various times after death. But Cox, following the Jainist model, which is also followed by various Buddhists, rejected those ideas for the "instantaneous" theory.

I suddenly remembered that the old man knows everything about everything. After all, religion was his game.

Am I telling you what you already know?

Not the specifics. Tell me more. What about "twenty-five years"?

Cox believed, like many Hindus, like many Buddhists, that a child should not be confronted with the specifics of his/her previous life until it's already been "reacclimated" to the world. This is especially true in the West, but even in the East, where the kids grow up fully accepting the notion of reincarnation, it's believed that the specifics of their past lives should never be revealed until adulthood.

So Sykes was fifteen at the time of Tory's death. If he found his soulmate and waited twenty-five years, he'd be forty years old. If the young woman accepted him, they'd be forty and twenty-five with a second chance at life.

Yes, at love.

Yes, at love.

One more thing. Cox believed that dying persons, if their love was strong enough, could influence *where* they'd be reincarnated.

So Tory would be reborn at the exact moment of her death, somewhere in the metro area, as she said on her deathbed, "I won't be far."

Exactly, so Sykes, with all his money, spent the last twenty-five years tracking down every young girl born at exactly 11:58 p.m. on August 29, 1990, somewhere in New Jersey, or nearby areas in New York, Connecticut, and Pennsylvania.

How many did he find?

Twenty-seven. Twenty-seven "prospects." And he stalked every single one of them. Legal records, medical records, school records. He also took photos of them at various ages, and he hired several unscrupulous PIs to help him out. He even snuck into their bedrooms and photographed pages from their diaries.

He was deranged.

Yes.

Why did he bother going to school?

Because of Ian Stevenson.

The paranormal guy at the University of Virginia?

Yes, I neglected to mention that he was a world-class "expert" on reincarnation.

"Neglected"? Not really. You think you're quite the clever storyteller.

I'm trying.

Stevenson was the founder of the university's Division of Perceptual Studies, and he traveled all over the world researching metempsychosis, with countless trips to India. His biggest books were *Twenty Cases Suggestive of Reincarnation*, 1966, and *Reincarnation and Biology*, 1997. Despite his fame, he was mostly ignored by the scientific community, who claimed that his research was mostly anecdotal, full of leading questions, and endlessly confabulated. One of his most significant theories was the belief that birthmarks and birth defects can be transferred from one life to the next.

Which could help Sykes narrow his pool.

Exactly. Tory had unusual amber eyes, and she also had a PDA at birth. So did the first three young women he approached: Wendy Nelson, Camille Anderson, and Chloe Hathaway.

And Zoe Hathaway?

Yes.

So why did Camille go off the rails?

Because she believed that she loved him. Because she also truly believed, and *still* believes, that she's the "one."

The reincarnated Tory.

Yes, but for some unknown reason, Sykes decided she wasn't, so he moved on to Chloe, who, it seems, he thought was the "real" one. But I suspect he also wanted to take a look at Zoe. After all, they're identicals.

Which means, in the end, it was simple jealousy?

I don't know how "simple" it was, but Camille made up her mind to eliminate the only rivals she knew she had. Or assumed she had. Even poor Wendy, who was no longer in the picture. Whom she shot in a parking lot. But she got a lot more creative with Chloe, mutilating her amber eyes and writing "Not Her" across her forehead.

Then she went after Zoe.

Yes, even after Sykes's was dead. In her mind, Zoe was *still* a rival, a possible "Tory," and Camille wanted her both dead and mutilated. When I asked her why, especially after Sykes had killed himself, she said, "You're too stupid to understand."

A young woman of perception.

I laughed at the old cadaver.

Killing Zoe was her final mission. Then she was planning to kill herself and join Sykes in the "great beyond," the great sorrowful cycle of saṃsāra.

How did she get into the building?

It seems she bribed the guard at the metal detector. Fifty thousand dollars! Money was no object. When I got there, I tased the same guy, and I felt bad about it. When I learned what he'd done, I wanted to tase him again.

Now what happens?

What do you mean "what happens?"? Camille goes off to Bedford Hills for the rest of her life.

I meant you and Zoe.

I know what you meant.

Well?

I shrugged.

I have no idea. She wants to quit the agency and work for me.

You're simply irresistible.

You don't approve?

What do I know? I'm a billion years old, and I live in a stone tower, and I can't even walk across the room. Maybe you two are falling in love with each other. What do I know?

I wish *somebody* knew.

34. Tennis

Wednesday, May 18th
61°

S HE WAS playing tennis.
Of course, she was.

I bet she plays second or third singles on the Princeton women's team. With her graceful yet zipless serves, her powerfully accurate ground strokes, her seemingly non-existent volley game. She was currently in the process of demolishing a hapless opponent, an undersized male withering in the late afternoon sun.

I was sitting on a nearby bench, reading over the appendix to the Cox book, which summarized the several-thousand-year background on moksha, karma, and the liberation from saṃsāra. In which Dr. Singh believes. In which, as he put it, "half the world" believes. Hindus, Jains, Buddhists, Sikhs, and Manicheans. Even a bunch of quirky westerners. Gnostics, Basilides, the heretical Cathars, the Rosicrucians, American Transcendentalists (whom I never cared for), as well as Blavatsky and her Theosophists.

Not to mention nutty Schopenhauer, not to mention even nuttier Nietzsche.

Even Voltaire (another one of my *not* favorites):

"The doctrine of metempsychosis is, above all, neither absurd nor useless."

And, of course, the New Ager Debbie Blake.

Even the Greeks took a stab at it, especially Pythagoras, who apparently coined the term "metempsychosis," as well as Plato in the *Phaedo* and elsewhere. Mighty Augustine, of course, condemned the idea in *The City of God*. As for me, I have trouble seeing the world around me as nothing but a "suffering-laden" endless cycle to be liberated from. I happen to enjoy things the way they are, both the good and the bad. Besides, if I ever did "come back," I'd want to come back as me. Which, apparently, is impossible. But, to some extent, I "get" Sykes's obsession. If you love somebody like *he* loved, like Poe describes, with "a love that's more than love," then maybe nothing else matters. Maybe you'll be willing to clutch at any straw available. Maybe you'll read a short, obscure book and spend the entire rest of your life endlessly searching for amber-eyed girls.

I shut the book.

Speaking of Poe, he used variations on the theme in several of his stories, which, of course, doesn't mean that he *believed* it. "Morella," "The Oval Portrait," and "Metzengerstein." Even "Ligeia," his second-best story, one of my favorites, is a Poeesque variation on the transmigration theme.

Then I thought about the various movies, none of which had been able to do very much with the concept: *Audrey Rose* (probably the best), *The Reincarnation of Peter Proud*, *I Origins*, Shimizu's boring *Rinni* (*Reincarnation*), and the 1956 forerunner, *Bridey Murphy*, starring Teresa Wright. Which was based on the sensationalist 1956 book by hypnotist Morey Bernstein about how he dropped a Colorado housewife, Virginia Tighe, into "hypnotic regression," where she suddenly remembered all kinds of stuff about a past life as "Bridey Murphy" in Cork, Ireland. Most of which proved to be historically untrue.

Even Tighe eventually came to believe it was bogus.

Maybe the best filmic approach to the theme, although nobody seems to agree with me, was the *X-Files* episode "Born Again," about the little girl who's actually the reincarnation of a murdered detective, who's back for revenge.

Go girl.

Did I ever mention that I'm a bit of an *X-Files* buff?

In the end, I prefer the famous Faulkner quote, which has nothing to do with reincarnation:

> *The past is never dead. It's not even past.*

The tennis match was over.

I watched her offer a few consoling words to the guy she'd just crushed.

What's the line in the Betjeman poem about the wimpy guy who gets his ass whipped by the girl he's in love with?

> *The warm-handled racket is back in its press,*
> *But my shock-headed victor, she loves me no less.*

Well, this little guy in Ridgewood wasn't about to get any "lovin'" from Kimberly Watts.

No chance.

As mentioned, I was sitting on a nearby bench, within the thirty beautiful acres of the upscale Upper Ridgewood Tennis Club, founded in 1914, now a state-of-the-art tennis facility for the upper class.

She walked over.

She'd seen me arrive earlier.

"Did you enjoy the show?"

"Why don't you pick on somebody your own size."

She laughed.

She was tall, tanned, wealthy, athletic, and covered with a sheen of sweat that glistened in the fading sunlight. She wore traditional whites, which I liked. Even the headband that held her long blonde hair in place was white. All in all, she was a very pretty, young woman, very "entitled," and she knew it, and she didn't mind at all.

Her lovely whites contrasted sharply with Cortez's orange, which still lingered in my mind. After a long morning with the feds and NYPD in Manhattan, I came straight back to Paterson and stopped at the Passaic County jail to talk to the peabrain who'd "confessed" to hanging the father of the tennis player's boyfriend.

"Who paid you off?"

"F— you."

Actually, it was two distinct words, said rather dismissively.

But I knew what I needed to know.

"How's your shoulder?" I said, referring to the memory of Poison, the deceased pit bull.

"You're Savannah's cop," Kimberly remembered.

"Private cop."

"Ahh."

"How long have you been going out with Daniel?"

"Two months, but the judge never liked me."

"Why?"

"He thought I was stuck-up."

"Are you?"

"Yes, a lot of the time, but it's over anyway."

"You and Daniel?"

"Yes."

"Why?"

She shrugged as if a faded romance at her age meant next to nothing.

After all, the world was at her feet.

"He's gotten a bit too weird. Besides, I think he's still got the hots for Angela."

I was surprised.

To say the least.

"He had a thing for Angela?" I repeated rather stupidly.

She didn't seem to mind.

"Yeah."

"When?"

"A few months ago, at the end of last year."

"Did Savannah know?"

She laughed.

"Of course not."

"Did you ever see a film called *Secret in Their Eyes*?"

"Never heard of it."

She was standing in front of me. A bit of a goddess in the twilight.

"Are we done? I want to burn off another one of these losers before I go home."

"Do you have any friends?" I asked rudely.

She smiled, as if she liked the question.

"Millions. They all want to be just like me."

There was something almost admirable about her honesty, about her colossal arrogance.

When she walked away, my cell vibrated.

It was Nonna.

"I'm at your service."

She ignored me.

"Have you seen the editorial in the *Star-Ledger*?"

"No."

"It's about the judge, written by Savannah. Are you sure that girl's down in Jamaica?"

She was worried.

So was I.

"Let me find out."

We hung up, and I dialed Savannah.

It went direct to voicemail.

"It's Savannah. I hope you're having a lovely day. Please tell me how you're doing."

35. Pines Lake

Wednesday, May 18th
58°

THERE WAS a noose around her neck.

With blood dripping down the side of her face.

She looked barely conscious.

Daniel turned around when I kicked in the front door. He had some kind of Ruger tucked in his belt, which he pulled out and aimed at my face.

He was—how should I describe it?—looking pretty "unhinged."

Deranged.

Maybe he and Camille could connect on psychomatch.com?

I shot him through the right shoulder, and he flew back to the hardwood floor, still holding his Ruger.

I walked over.

"Do I need to shoot you again?"

"No, that'll do."

"Toss the gun."

He did.

"Don't you know," I wondered, unable to resist, "that Cortez confessed?"

"Who cares?"

He certainly didn't.

I removed the noose from Savannah's neck and called Luca.

Savannah, gradually reviving, was still sitting on the floor. She looked over at her brother and asked the obvious question, which I already knew the answer to.

"Why?"

"Because the bastard was screwing my girlfriend! Because you wouldn't leave things alone!"

Which clearly referred to the editorial in today's *Ledger* that explained the whole "András Papp in the basement" business in, of course, the best possible light.

I had Nonna read it to me while I was racing from Ridgewood to Pines Lake. It made him sound like a no-brainer for sainthood. A good and decent man who'd provided András Papp with the only thing he wanted in this life. Punishment for his crime. A chance at retribution, at reparation.

I guess it didn't go over so well with the brother.

Savannah was still working on the "girlfriend" reference.

Shocked.

Visibly.

"Kimberly?"

Daniel sneered. Sorry, but it's the most accurate word I can come up with.

"You're such a moron, Savannah. You've never had a clue."

He was right.

She didn't.

So he told her.

Maliciously.

"Angela."

She was shocked all over again.

Into silence.

I decided to get involved in the brother/sister back-and-forth.

"How did you know for sure?"

Daniel looked at me as though he felt sorry for me. As though I was even stupider than his sister.

"Because I caught them in bed."

He looked at his sister and clarified.

"Naked!"

"When?" I tried.

"In January. Which was about a month after I discovered that there was some guy in a jail cell hidden in my father's secret basement. Which I discovered when Travis left the door open."

"What did your father say?"

"He lied, of course. What else?"

"Tell me."

"He said it was some kind of "scared-straight" isolation program. He looked at me and said, 'Trust me.'"

"Did you?"

"Of course not, but he was my father, and I thought I loved him, so I let it go. I kept my mouth shut."

"Until Angela."

"Until Angela."

"When you started blackmailing your own father."

"Yes."

Forcing the judge to send money to the Innocence Project to cast suspicion on both Angela and Greco's wife, who volunteered there.

"Until you decided to kill him."

"Yes."

"You might want to press on that wound a little bit."

"Maybe I prefer to bleed out."

"Fine with me."

Savannah was still mulling over the fact that her best friend had had affairs with both her brother and her father. And that she had absolutely no idea.

I could hear the sirens approaching.

"Angela?" she said as if to herself.

In disbelief.

"Yes, you stupid idiot."

36. St. Joe's

I FELT LIKE CRAP.

An alien feeling for me.

Yeah, I'd managed to "solve" two cases, but another girl was in the hospital.

St. Joe's in Wayne.

On Hamburg Turnpike.

Earlier, her brother had lured her to their house in Pines Lake, then clocked her in the head with his Ruger. Now she was lying in a hospital bed with a severe concussion, with a white bandage on her head.

She'd lost her father. Now she'd lost her brother. Who knows, maybe she'll even lose her best friend.

Even when you finally figure things out, you always feel like you took too much time. Like you might have been able to prevent something. But, to tell the truth, the feeling doesn't last too long. What's the point? I did my best, and it's all over now.

Same with the Chloe Hathaway case.

Savannah stirred, a bit drowsy, drugged with something.

She looked up at me. It was hard to ignore how pretty she was, even with her head bashed in.

"What *are* we, Colt?"

Not, where's my brother?

Not, who won the Mets game?

Not, what's the weather like outside?

But, what *are* we?

"What would you like us to be?" I said.

It was a lousy answer. It wasn't even a real answer.

Maybe I should go live at the top of Stone Tower with my great-great-uncle and never come out again.

She didn't take offense.

"I don't know," she said.

She said it thoughtfully.

"We'll figure it out," I said.

Which I said without the slightest conviction that I could ever "figure" it out. Or figure out Zoe. Or Roxs. Or Rikki O'Brien, the girl from Cape May two months ago. All of whom deserved a whole lot better than me.

Which I don't say with some kind of self-effacing sense of self-demeaning modesty. I've got nothing but confidence about myself. I *know* myself. Thank you, Socrates.

Except in regards to the irresistible sex.

"What time is it?"

I looked at my watch.

"Just past midnight."

"You can go home, Colt. I think I'm stoned anyway."

I laughed.

"Are you sleepy?"

"Like Snow White after the apple."

I laughed again.

"Kiss me before you go."

I bent over and did as commanded.

Why are women so delicious?

Am I allowed to say that?

I felt better.

Which was all her doing.

Outside in the parking lot, I was heading to my car when Vinnie Ravello stepped out of the darkness. What is it with these mob guys and the darkness of the night? Suddenly, I felt crappy again.

"Get lost, Vinnie."

He didn't move.

"The don wants a word."

He nodded his head, as only New Jersey Italians can do, and I saw the black Town Car, with the blackout windows, idling nearby and waiting just for me.

When I walked over, a soldier in a designer suit opened the back door, and I got inside next to the don. It seemed as though I was twice as big as the most powerful man in North Jersey.

"I pay my debts," he said.

Handing me an envelope.

It's *always* an envelope.

A thick one.

"I don't want it."

Never a good thing to say to the mob.

"Besides," I explained, "Angela's affair with the judge will probably come out in the wash."

"But not the other thing."

Meaning Angela's parentage.

Which is what everything was all about anyway.

The don was still holding out the money.

"I'm not taking it."

He put it down on the seat between us.

Expressionless.

"I owe you," he said.

"We're even."

He paid no attention. Then he almost-but-not-quite smiled.

"You thought *I* did it."

Meaning the murder of Judge Garvey.

"Briefly," I admitted. "And I'm sure you bought off Cortez."

"He's better off the streets. Besides, his mother is happy."

"Yeah, a condo in Hillcrest is quite an upgrade from her previous dump."

"I like moms," he said.

I suspected it was true.

Then I decided to stick my nose into something no one should ever mess around with.

The family's "personal" matters.

"Shouldn't Angela know who she is?"

He didn't seem angry.

"Would *you* tell her, Jack?"

"I would. I believe in the truth."

"Just like your uncle Tom."

"Exactly."

"Think about it, Jack. Would you really want such an innocent young girl getting involved with the likes of me? Involved in the kind of life I lead? That my family leads?"

I didn't respond.

Maybe Ravello was right.

We left it right where it was.

"I like you, Jack."

"I don't like you."

"Fine. I'm fine with that."

I got out of the car, nodded at Vinnie, and walked off into the darkness.

Away from the darkness.

37. Drumthwacket

Y OU'VE BEEN busy, Jack."

"It's not quite over."

I was standing in the private wood-paneled library on the second floor of the governor's mansion in Princeton.

On Stockton Street.

"I figured as much."

I put the Mauser M18 hunting rifle on the wooden table. It was still inside the green trash bag.

Keith Hopkins was the oddly popular governor of the Garden State. A fiscally frugal Democrat, he was efficient, effective, and a sympathy-inducing tragic figure. Having had two crazy daughters, both now deceased.

"Would you like to sit, Jack?"

"I won't be long."

I handed him the recording.

"It's the confession of the man who killed Meredith. His name is Eric Marker, and he lives on Sandstorm Lane in Scottsdale.

"Bryan's brother?" he said, surprised.

"Younger brother."

When he thought about it, he was no longer surprised.

"I guess we both know why," he said.

"Yes, she destroyed his older brother."

He didn't disagree.

"I considered," I admitted, "leaving it alone."

He understood.

"Why didn't you, Jack?"

"Because it's murder, and you can't look away from that."

"Thanks, Jack."

"I'm going home."

We shook hands.

Out in the corridor, she was waiting for me, the First Lady, in a soft, white bathrobe, mostly open, radiating sexual heats like an exploding sun.

"Thanks, Jack. I knew you would."

I didn't say a word.

I left Drumthwacket through the back garden.

The Jersey night was cool and clear and quiet and beautiful. Perfect. But I still had some lingering crap I needed to wash away.

Or blast away.

I got in my XTS and put on the Boss again.

Loud.

"Born to Run."

The best.

New Jersey has absolutely everything, but, oddly enough, it doesn't have a "state song."

I nominate BTR.

Wendy, let me in, I wanna be your friend
I want to guard your dreams and visions.

I hit the New Jersey byways, cruising Route 27 to 95 to the Garden State.

It was good to be a Jersey boy.

Oh, honey, tramps like us,
Baby, we were born to run.

William Baer, a recent Guggenheim fellow, is the author of twenty-two books including *New Jersey Noir*; *Times Square and Other Stories*; *One-and-Twenty Tales*; *Companion*; *The Ballad Rode into Town*; *Formal Salutations: New & Selected Poems*; *Classic American Films*; and *The Unfortunates* (recipient of the T.S. Eliot Award). A former Fulbright in Portugal, he's also received the Jack Nicholson Screenwriting Award and a Creative Writing Fellowship in fiction from the National Endowment for the Arts.

ALSO FROM ABLE MUSE PRESS

Jacob M. Appel, *The Cynic in Extremis: Poems*

William Baer, *Times Square and Other Stories;*
    New Jersey Noir: A Novel;
    New Jersey Noir (Cape May): A Novel;
    New Jersey Noir (Barnegat Light):A Novel

Lee Harlin Bahan, *A Year of Mourning (Petrarch): Translation*

Melissa Balmain, *Walking in on People (Able Muse Book Award for Poetry)*

Ben Berman, *Strange Borderlands: Poems; Figuring in the Figure: Poems*

David Berman, *Progressions of the Mind: Poems*

Lorna Knowles Blake, *Green Hill (Able Muse Book Award for Poetry)*

Michael Cantor, *Life in the Second Circle: Poems*

Catherine Chandler, *Lines of Flight: Poems*

William Conelly, *Uncontested Grounds: Poems*

Maryann Corbett, *Credo for the Checkout Line in Winter: Poems;*
    Street View: Poems; In Code: Poems

Will Cordeiro, *Trap Street (Able Muse Book Award for Poetry)*

Brian Culhane, *Remembering Lethe: Poems*

John Philip Drury, *Sea Level Rising: Poems*

Rhina P. Espaillat, *And After All: Poems*

Anna M. Evans, *Under Dark Waters: Surviving the* Titanic*: Poems*

Stephen Gibson, *Frida Kahlo in Fort Lauderdale: Poems*

D. R. Goodman, *Greed: A Confession: Poems*

Carrie Green, *Studies of Familiar Birds: Poems*

Margaret Ann Griffiths, *Grasshopper: The Poetry of M A Griffiths*

Janis Harrington, *How to Cut a Woman in Half: Poems*

Katie Hartsock, *Bed of Impatiens: Poems*

Elise Hempel, *Second Rain: Poems*

Jan D. Hodge, *Taking Shape: Carmina figurata;*
    The Bard & Scheherazade Keep Company: Poems

Ellen Kaufman, *House Music: Poems; Double-Parked, with Tosca: Poems*

Len Krisak, *Say What You Will (Able Muse Book Award for Poetry)*

Emily Leithauser, *The Borrowed World (Able Muse Book Award for Poetry)*

Hailey Leithauser, *Saint Worm: Poems*

Carol Light, *Heaven from Steam: Poems*

Kate Light, *Character Shoes: Poems*

April Lindner, *This Bed Our Bodies Shaped: Poems*

Martin McGovern, *Bad Fame: Poems*

Jeredith Merrin, *Cup: Poems*

Richard Moore, *Selected Poems;*
    The Rule That Liberates: An Expanded Edition: Selected Essays

Richard Newman, *All the Wasted Beauty of the World: Poems*

Alfred Nicol, *Animal Psalms: Poems*

Deirdre O'Connor, *The Cupped Field (Able Muse Book Award for Poetry)*

Frank Osen, *Virtue, Big as Sin (Able Muse Book Award for Poetry)*

Alexander Pepple (Editor), *Able Muse Anthology;*
    Able Muse: A Review of Poetry, Prose & Art (semiannual, winter 2010 on)

James Pollock, *Sailing to Babylon: Poems*

Aaron Poochigian, *The Cosmic Purr: Poems; Manhattanite*
    (Able Muse Book Award for Poetry)

Tatiana Forero Puerta, *Cleaning the Ghost Room: Poems*

Jennifer Reeser, *Indigenous: Poems; Strong Feather: Poems*

John Ridland, *Sir Gawain and the Green Knight (Anonymous): Translation;*
    Pearl (Anonymous): Translation

Stephen Scaer, *Pumpkin Chucking: Poems*

Hollis Seamon, *Corporeality: Stories*

Ed Shacklee, *The Blind Loon: A Bestiary*

Carrie Shipers, *Cause for Concern (Able Muse Book Award for Poetry)*

Matthew Buckley Smith, *Dirge for an Imaginary World*
    (Able Muse Book Award for Poetry)

Susan de Sola, *Frozen Charlotte: Poems*

Barbara Ellen Sorensen, *Compositions of the Dead Playing Flutes: Poems*

Rebecca Starks, *Time Is Always Now: Poems; Fetch, Muse: Poems*

Sally Thomas, *Motherland: Poems*

Paulette Demers Turco (Editor), *The Powow River Poets Anthology II*

Rosemerry Wahtola Trommer, *Naked for Tea: Poems*

Wendy Videlock, *Wise to the West: Poems; Slingshots and Love Plums: Poems;*
    The Dark Gnu and Other Poems; Nevertheless: Poems

Richard Wakefield, *A Vertical Mile: Poems; Terminal Park: Poems*

Gail White, *Asperity Street: Poems*

Chelsea Woodard, *Vellum: Poems*

Rob Wright, *Last Wishes: Poems*

www.ablemusepress.com

CPSIA information can be obtained
at www.ICGtesting.com
Printed in the USA
BVHW040744070523
663731BV00020B/350

9 781773 490991